ALLIGATOR WARRIOR
HALPATTER
TUSTENUGGEE

BY

L L EADIE

ILLUSTRATIONS BY L L EADIE

Publisher Dolly Dimple Ink
Lake City, Florida

ISBN-13: 978-1-7347371-2-7

Libracy of Congress Control No:

Table of Contents

Part I -The Green Corn Dance: "What's in a Name?"

Chapter I - A Child of the Big Lake (Lake Halpatter)

Once upon a time there lived a little Seminole boy, who grew up to become a very important warrior. When he was just a baby his family left Georgia and moved to Florida, the village of many Indians. North Florida was an Indian's paradise. There were plenty of lakes, rivers, animals, land, and few white settlers. Most of the white settlers were Spanish and traded fairly with the Indians. This Seminole boy's family lived happily in an Indian village along the banks of a big lake. Sadly, their happiness did not last. For most of his life he would fight for a happy place to live once again.

Our story begins in that Seminole Indian village later known as Alligator Town (Halpata Tolophka). The sun is rising in the east over the big lake and the little Indian boy named Little Voice Standing Small and his mother are just rising too.

"Mother are you awake?" asked Little Voice Standing Small from his hammock.

"Yes," answered his mother.

"When is the Green Corn Dance?"

"The medicine man will decide soon. The corn is almost ready to harvest. The Green Corn Dance will happen during the 'little moon in June,'" explained his mother from her hammock.

"Do you think, at this Green Corn Dance, I will become a man?" asked Little Voice Standing Small hopefully.

"You know, Little Voice Standing Small, that your uncle, not me, will decide when you are ready for manhood," answered his mother as she got up and went outside. "Now come and help me, little man, roll another log into the fire. I need to start cooking," smiled his mother.

"Yes, mother," said Little Voice Standing Small as he left their wooden hut and helped build his mother's fire. "I am going turkey hunting today with Little Big Fat."

"Good, maybe we will eat something besides squirrel stew today," laughed his mother.

"Mother, I am thirteen years old now. I may kill a black bear today," exclaimed Little Voice Standing Small.

"Maybe a deer too!" teased his mother as she hung her iron kettle over the fire.

"I wonder what my new name will be," said Little Voice Standing Small as he sat on a fireside log and ate a piece of coontie bread.

"How about, 'Smells Like Urine?'" laughed Little Big Fat as he walked up to their fire. Little Big Fat was built short, like Little Voice Standing Small, but he was stout.

"Hello, Little Big Fat. Are you ready to go turkey hunting or are you still hungry?" teased Little Voice Standing Small as he looked at his friend eyeing their food.

The two Seminole boys were best friends. In fact, they had a "fellowhood." This meant they had agreed to be friends for life. They would protect one another from all harm. The boys were the same age, and both hoped to become men at the Green Corn Dance.

"I told my mother that we would kill a black bear today," said Little Voice Standing Small, smiling. as they followed the tree shaded path around the big lake. It was a beautiful clear warm day. There was plenty of wildlife living all around the lake.

Little Big Fat just laughed at his good friend's wishes.

"You don't think I could do it, do you? I'm not afraid of a black bear!" exclaimed Little Voice Standing Small as he drew his bow string tight with an arrow and pretended to see a wild animal. "I could stop him or *any* big animal right in his tracks with just *one* arrow!"

"Little Big Fat laughed again at his good friend.

Suddenly...

"WATCH OUT!" warned Little Big Fat, who was not pretending.

There in the tall grass that grew along the shoreline was a huge bull alligator (halpata). Little Voice Standing Small turned just in time to see the alligator charge him! With his arrow already drawn, he shot it right into one of the alligator's eyes. The alligator stopped and then retreated back into hiding in the tall grass.

"Little Voice Standing Small, *you did it!* You stopped an alligator with just *one* arrow! What a good shot!" shouted the excited Little Big Fat.

Little Voice Standing Small said with a trembling voice, "Thank you Little Big Fat, for warning me!"

Although both Indian boys were scared, they had proved their bravery. That evening, as Little Voice Standing Small and his mother enjoyed eating his uncle's catch of big mouth bass, from the big lake, he learned of his new grown-up name.

"Did you hear Little Voice Standing Small, the fifteen sticks arrived today from the Medicine Man?" asked his uncle who was also eating with them by their campfire. His uncle fed the fire first before he ate; to prevent their fish from burning.

"No. Does that mean there are fifteen days until the Green Corn Dance?" asked Little Voice Standing Small anxiously.

"Yes," answered his uncle smiling at him.

"Brother, did you hear about Little Voice Standing Small's, and Little Big Fat's, meeting with an alligator today?" asked Little Voice Standing Small's mother as she took another bite of her fish.

"Yes," replied Little Voice Standing Small's uncle as he nodded his head and smiled at him. "That was a very wise shot, *Alligator (Halpatter)*."

"ALLIGATOR? Did you call me *Alligator,* uncle?" asked the confused Little Voice Standing Small.

"Yes. Your manhood name will be Alligator. I will introduce you to the Medicine Man, King Payne, and our Seminole band of elders as *Alligator* at the Green Corn Dance!"

Chapter II - The Marooned People

"There are still twelve days till the Green Corn Dance. I can't believe that only three days have passed, mother. It seems like three months!" exclaimed Little Voice Standing Small, as he lay in his hammock wide awake.

"Waiting is always difficult, my son. Be patient," said Little Voice Standing Small's mother and then she yawned.

The sun had set a couple of hours earlier and it was getting late. Suddenly, there were strange sounds coming from outside their hut in the darkness.

"What was that?" asked the alarmed Little Voice Standing Small as he sat up and listened.

"I don't know," answered his mother uneasily, as she too listened. "Maybe, it's a black bear or a panther."

Little Voice Standing Small quickly, but quietly, got up, retrieved his bow and arrows, and headed for the door. He peered out into the darkness. The moon was not quite full, but still shone. He could see three figures by their campfire. They appeared to be eating, that day's leftover turtle stew, from the iron pot. Little Voice Standing Small did not recognize them. He crept quietly closer to the strangers. Little Voice Standing Small drew his arrow in his bow, and surprised them all, when he shouted, "WHO ARE YOU?" from behind a tall cypress tree.

"Please don't shoot!" cried out a scared woman and then there were children's cries too.

"Who are *you?*" demanded Little Voice Standing Small, trying to sound very grown up and stern.

"We are runaway slaves from Georgia. Please don't shoot us! We are just hungry and thirsty. We just need a place to rest and then we'll be on our way. We won't bother

7

you, and your family anymore," begged a boy about Little Voice Standing Small's age.

Little Voice Standing Small came out of his hiding place, but still had his bow drawn. He was not sure if he could really trust these strangers. He carefully walked up to the campfire and looked into their scared faces. Their eyes did not lie. He could now see the frightened woman holding a crying baby girl in her arms and another scared little girl by the hand. There was also a young man, about his age, standing in front of his mother and sisters. This boy was very brave, thought Little Voice Standing Small.

"Please, please don't hurt us!" cried the frightened woman.

"I won't hurt you," said Little Voice Standing Small in a much kinder voice now, as he lowered his bow. "Mother come out. It's safe. They are in need of food and drink."

Little Voice Standing Small's mother greeted the strangers like honored guests. She served her hungry late-night company coontie bread, box turtle stew, and corn soup drink called sofkee.

Little Voice Standing Small quickly made friends with the slave boy named Moses. That night the two boys slept by the campfire while the women and children slept comfortably in the hut. The two boys talked most of the night.

"In twelve days, I will become a man," said Little Voice Standing Small proudly. "My new name will be Alligator." Little Voice went on to explain to Moses how he earned his new name.

"You are very lucky to be a Seminole Indian," said Moses. "My people were stolen from their family. I do not know them. I would like a new family like yours!" Moses next told Little Voice Standing Small that his name, "Moses" meant that he was to lead his lost tribe and family out of slavery; just like the Moses had done in the good book.

"Tomorrow I will take you, Moses, to visit a Seminole band of Maroons," said Little Voice Standing Small. "Maybe, we will find some of your family tribe there."

In the morning, at breakfast, Little Voice Standing Small and his mother introduced the runaway slaves to their village. Everyone was very friendly to them. In fact, many brought gifts: Indian dolls for the little girls, bow and arrows for Moses, and a pretty looking glass for his mother.

"It's not safe for them here, Little Voice Standing Small. Soon the slave hunters will be looking for them," explained Little Voice Standing Small's uncle to him.

"You are right, Uncle. Soon the slave catchers will come with their dogs, and hunt Moses and his family down, like foxes in their den," said Little Voice Standing Small as the two of them sat by his uncle's hut.

"Yes. I am sorry, Little Voice Standing Small, but your new friend can not stay here with us. Have Moses and his family put on Seminole clothes and then bring me their old slave clothes. I will carry their clothes out with me to the center of the big lake and toss them in! The slave hunters' dogs won't find any trace of them here! Go now!" demanded his wise uncle.

Little Voice Standing Small helped Moses tie his gift of a colorful new handkerchief around his neck. He also showed him how to wrap his new turban around his head too. Moses then dressed in his new buckskin hunting shirt and knee-high moccasins. Moses studied his reflection in his mother's new looking glass mirror.

Little Voice Standing Small smiled at him and said, "Tell your mother to stay inside the hut today. She and your little sisters should stay out of sight. They will be safe here for now. My people will protect them. Are you ready to leave to find your new place, Moses – 'the one who leads his people?'"

"Yes! I look forward to meeting my new family," said Moses as he stood before Little Voice Standing Small looking like a proud Seminole Indian.

"I can't promise you a family, Moses. Hopefully, one of the Maroon tribesmen will want to marry your mother and adopt you and your sisters."

"Thank you, Little Voice Standing Small."

The boys left on two small horses. The Seminole village was a day's ride from Little Voice Standing Small's town.

Moses was very excited when they had finally reached the Maroon village after a long hot day's ride. The Maroon Indians welcomed Little Voice Standing Small and his new friend. Moses met many former slaves that were now Seminole Indians. They stayed the night, and in the morning a decision had been made by the Maroon leaders.

"Take these gifts to your mother. If she accepts them, bring her and your little sisters back to meet your mother's new husband, *and* your new father," explained a Maroon leader.

Moses's mother accepted the wedding gifts of a blue stone necklace and a woolen blanket. Moses and his family moved into their new home at the Maroon village. His new father prepared a feast from his hunt to welcome his new family. He gave Moses one of his gold earrings to welcome his new son. Moses's mother gave her new husband a buckskin hunting shirt that Little Voice Standing Small's mother had given to her, for him.

Now Moses and his family felt safe. Moses now had a real African tribe family. His dream of becoming a Seminole Maroon Indian had come true!

Chapter III - Staring Fear in the Eye of the One-Eyed Alligator

The moon was almost full. In two days the Green Corn Dance would begin. There were just two sticks left hanging in the Indian village. Little Voice Standing Small and his mother were preparing by gathering vegetables from their garden. Little Voice Standing Small had made a big decision.

"Mother, if I am to become a man in two days, I must prove it to myself."

"What do you mean, Little Voice Standing Small?" asked his mother.

"I must show the one-eyed alligator that I am not afraid of him!" exclaimed Little Voice Standing Small.

"Then you must seek a little person to carry with you. But be careful not to make him mad. And don't let him know if you are afraid of him...then no harm will come to you."

"Yes, mother, you are right, a little person would bring me good luck! I think I know where to find one. He is a clever one though. He hides under rocks, fallen trees, and inside the knotholes of the oldest oak trees. I will have to take a fish net to catch him. I could never catch him with my bare hands. He is as tricky as a rabbit!"

"Good luck to you, Little Voice Standing Small!" exclaimed his mother.

"Little Voice Standing Small headed out into the forest to look for his little good luck charm before he hunted for the one-eyed alligator. It must have been his lucky day because after rolling over only two logs he spotted the little person. Quickly, Little Voice Standing Small tossed the net over him.

"What is it? What do you want with me?" asked the angry little person from under the fishnet.

"My name is Little Voice Standing Small, but soon to be Alligator at the Green Corn Dance. I must seek the one-eyed alligator. Please don't be mad at me little man. I need your help."

"My name is not 'little man!' My name is Gold (Lani), and yes, I have seen the one-eyed alligator! He has an arrow sticking out of his eye. Did you shoot him?" asked Gold from under the net.

"Yes, I did. If you will be my good luck charm, I will give you a handful of stone beads," said Little Voice Standing Small, hopefully.

"Mmm...stone beads are nice...but...gold beads are even better!" said the clever little person, Gold, with a smile across his tiny face. *"I love gold!"*

"Little Voice Standing Small agreed, and then they were off together, in a canoe to seek the one-eyed alligator. Gold sat on Little Voice Standing Small's shoulder, and talked to him nonstop, as Little Voice Standing Small slowly paddled the canoe around the big lake.

"Little Voice Standing Small, did I tell you that I love gold? That is how I got my name – *'Gold!'*"

"Yes, you told me, you told me." It seemed to Little Voice Standing Small, that Gold, was as noisy as a hungry seagull at the beach. He may scare away the one-eyed alligator. Maybe, it was not a good idea to have brought him along, thought Little Voice Standing Small. "Shhh...stop talking!"

"Remember, Little Voice Standing Small, you are the one who kidnapped me! I am your lucky charm! LOOK! There! Over there is your one-eyed alligator sunning himself on the bank!" yelled Gold, pointing in that direction.

"Yes, I see him!" said Little Voice Standing Small excitedly, as he quickly paddled toward the bank.

"Don't get too close to him! He still has *one* good eye," warned Gold.

From a safe distance, Little Voice Standing Small, called out to the one-eyed alligator. "Hello! Do you remember me?"

"How could he forget you? I don't think he likes you," said Gold still perched on Little Voice Standing Small's shoulder.

"He sure looks mad, doesn't he?" said Little Voice Standing Small, as he looked at the glaring one-eyed alligator.

"What do you expect? Well, we've seen him...so...let's go. He doesn't look like he's in the mood for company right now."

"No. I need to help him," explained Little Voice Standing Small.

"Help the one-eyed alligator? Are you out of your mind? How can you help *him?"* asked the surprised little person, Gold.

"I will take the arrow out of his blind eye," explained Little Voice Standing Small as he paddled the canoe up onto the sandy bank.

"WHOA! If you're short on arrows, I can lend you some! Are you sure you really want to lose *your* right hand today?" asked Gold as he climbed down from Little Voice Standing Small's shoulder and hid on the floor of the canoe.

"That's why I brought you, Gold! You are my lucky charm," said Little Voice Standing Small, as he stepped out onto the sandy beach. The scared little person, Gold peeked over the side of the canoe.

"The one-eyed alligator did not move but kept his one good eye on Little Voice Standing Small.

"You would have hurt me, if I had not shot you," explained Little Voice Standing Small, to the one-eyed alligator, as he slowly, very slowly, walked up to him.

"Aren't you afraid I will try to hurt you again?" asked the one-eyed alligator.

"I am no longer afraid of you. And I am not here to hurt you, or even to wrestle you, or to put you to sleep on your back either," said Little Voice Standing Small.

"Then, why are you here?" asked the one-eyed alligator.

"I am sorry I blinded you, alligator. I am here to remove my arrow from your blind eye," explained Little Voice Standing Small.

"And prove that you are a man?" asked the one-eyed alligator who knew the ways of the Seminoles.

"Yes. I will be honored to take your name, Alligator, at the Green Corn Dance," answered Little Voice Standing Small.

The one-eyed alligator never moved as Little Voice Standing Small removed the arrow, which had taken his sight, and nagged him for so many days. Little Voice Standing Small wondered now who the brave one truly was? Was it really him *or* was it the one-eyed alligator? Thank you was all the one-eyed alligator said. And then, Little Voice Standing Small, returned to the canoe to find that Gold had run away. However, all Little Voice Standing

Small could think about now, was that in two days, he would be known as *Alligator*!

Chapter IV - Let the Powwow Begin

The sun was just rising above the big lake's east side. Little Voice Standing Small smiled as he watched the last stick being taken down. Today was the day he had been waiting for – the first day of the Green Corn Dance. He quickly ran home to pack his belongings.

"Mother, are you ready to go?" asked the anxious Little Voice Standing Small as he picked up his stuffed buckskin bag.

"Slow down, Little Voice Standing Small, and come and help me pack. We must not forget the green corn," answered his mother with a smile. She knew how excited her son was.

"Yes, I will carry the green corn. Hurry mother! Our village will be leaving soon!" exclaimed Little Voice Standing Small. It seemed to him that his mother was moving as slow as a turtle walking across the hot sands.

She looked up at him with a smile and said, "Don't worry, Little Voice Standing Small, I will be ready. I would not miss *this* Green Corn Dance!"

"Nor would I!" laughed Little Voice Standing Small.

By the time the sun sat directly overhead in the clear blue sky, his village had arrived at this year's Green Corn Dance site. This was a place where no Seminoles lived. Many Seminole bands had already arrived, and more were on their way. There was much to do to get ready for the Green Corn Dance.

"Little Big Fat come help me remove the branches on the tall tree," said Little Voice Standing Small as he tucked his hatchet under the belt he wore and took off running in the direction of the tall thin tree.

Other Seminole boys were already climbing the tree and cutting off the branches for a ball game. Little Big Fat raced far behind Little Voice Standing Small. He ran as fast as he could, but he could not catch up with him. By the time he reached the tree he was out of breath.

Huffing and puffing Little Big Fat said, "Did we...have...to run...the entire way?"

"Come on Little Big Fat, give me a hand up this tree," said Little Voice Standing Small smiling at his good friend who was not much taller than him.

Little Big Fat lifted Little Voice Standing Small up so he could reach the branches to cut off. Soon they were playing ball with the other boys.

Several hours later the Seminole Indian chief, King Payne and his band had arrived.

"Boys, come and greet Chief Payne and his family," said Little Voice Standing Small's uncle.

The boys shook arms with their important guests. "You are come," they said in the Seminole way of greeting.

19

King Payne's two nephews, Blowing Wind and Sitting Frog joined the boys playing ball.

Later that evening at dusk, everyone gathered around the dance fire.

"Little Voice Standing Small, look over there...across the dance fire...at...at...at"

"What is it, Little Big Fat?" asked Little Voice Standing Small.

"That girl...do you see *that* girl?"

"Yes, there are lots of girls over there," laughed Little Voice Standing Small.

"The *one* that is talking to your mother. Do you know her?" asked Little Big Fat hopefully.

"Yes, her name is 'Hush Be Quiet'," laughed Little Voice Standing Small.

"Really? Hush Be Quiet? Why do they call her that?"

"I don't know. Maybe, because she is as loud as a croaking tree frog calling a summer shower," laughed Little Voice Standing Small.

"Mmm...I think I will dance with her. I won't have to worry about what to talk about, *will I?*" laughed Little Big Fat.

"She may dance with someone else," said Little Voice Standing Small.

"You are right, Little Voice Standing Small. Good idea. *You,* dance with her!" laughed Little Big Fat.

"What? I don't want to dance with her! You're the one looking at her!"

"Yes, that's why they call this dance, 'Steal a Partner,'" laughed Little Big Fat.

So being the good friend that he was, Little Voice Standing Small asked Hush Be Quiet to dance. And just as

Little Big Fat promised, he stole Hush Be Quiet from him, by pulling her gently away from Little Voice Standing Small. Much, much later Little Big Fat would marry Hush Be Quiet.

The next dance was called "the alligator" and Little Voice Standing Small was sure to join in on this line dance. He mimicked the one-eyed alligator by charging like him out of the tall grass.

The last dance of the evening was called the "old man's dance." The boys, who would soon be men, danced around the fire.

"Watch out, Little Big Fat," advised Little Voice Standing Small as they danced.

"Why? What is it?" asked the alarmed Little Big Fat, who was now looking around as he danced.

"Be ready to run fast," whispered Little Voice Standing Small.

All at once there were strange noises coming from the dark woods on the edge of the camp.

"What was that?" asked the scared Little Big Fat.

"I don't know. It could be a black bear or a wild dog. But, whatever it is, don't act scared! It could be a trick to see if we are truly brave," explained Little Voice Standing Small.

The drums, flutes, and the turtle shell rattles continued to play as all the boys danced in the light of the fire.

Suddenly, scary creatures began running out of the shadows and chasing the boys! Little Voice Standing Small escaped, but Little Big Fat, who was slower, was caught by the creatures and dragged into the darkness!

Little Voice Standing Small ran into the black forest to find his friend. His heart pounded like the drum as he ran through the darkness following the scary growling noises. Tree branches scratched his face as he ran quickly towards the strange sounds.

"GRRR!" growled a scary creature right behind him.

"AHHH!" yelled the surprised Little Voice Standing Small.

"It's just me!" laughed Little Big Fat, as he took off the scary mask that the old men had been wearing. "I think I passed their test of bravery... and so have you!"

Chapter V - Caught "Lying on the Ground Creeping" Red-Handed

The second day of the Green Corn Dance was known as the "picnic day." That was because there was plenty of good food and games to play. One of the most popular games was called, "little brother of war." It was a contest between the Indian villages.

"Moses? Is that you?" asked Little Voice Standing Small as his village took the field to play against the Seminole Maroon village.

"Hello, Little Voice Standing Small!" exclaimed Moses with a big smile.

"You are come," greeted Little Voice Standing Small as they shook arms. The boys were very happy to see one another.

"I now have a family, thanks to you! Maybe at the next Green Corn Dance, I too, will become a man. I know that you, Little Voice Standing Small, will become one of the great Seminole warriors!"

"Thank you, Moses. I am happy, that you are so happy!"

That evening Little Voice Standing Small couldn't sleep for thinking about what would happen tomorrow when he would be named Alligator. He decided to lay by the fire. He laid his head back on one of the extended logs and closed his eyes. But sleep still failed him. He laid there listening to the crickets chirping and a distant owl hooing. Suddenly there was a new sound. The sound was that of footsteps. Little Voice Standing Small listened very carefully. Was he in danger? Was it a friend or an animal creeping in the darkness? Whatever it was, it was getting closer and closer. He could now tell that it walked on four legs, not two. Was it a black bear or a wildcat? Then the steps stopped! Was

23

this wild animal looking at him from its hiding place? Would he be attacked? Little Voice Standing Small thought to himself, "I must be brave!" However, what he finally saw was a man crawling on all fours on the ground. He was stealing the Indian's valuables. Little Voice Standing Small jumped up and surprised the thief, who thought Little Voice Standing Small was asleep.

"You there, STOP!" shouted Little Voice Standing Small as he sprung to his feet.

The startled man tried to get up and run away, but he tripped over a log in the darkness and fell to the ground.

All this commotion woke up the Seminole camp. The thief was caught, and the belongings were returned to their owners.

Once again, Little Voice Standing Small had proved his bravery. He would soon become a man named Alligator!

Chapter VI - Fast, Here Comes the Judgement Day

"**I** am so proud of you, Little Voice Standing Small. As a boy you never complained about your chores such as finding firewood everyday. Soon, you will become a man. You won't need your mother to care for you anymore," said his mother with tears in her eyes.

Little Voice Standing Small hugged his mother and said, "I will take care of you now."

At dawn, the fasting began for the men. They could not eat anything until the next morning. The boys began cooking the black drink over the open fire.

"This stuff smells awful!" said Little Big Fat holding his nose as he stirred the black drink.

"You mean it doesn't make you hungry?" laughed Little Voice Standing Small teasing the always hungry Little Big Fat.

"LOOK! The Medicine Man has brought out the medicine bundle from its hiding place. He's hanging it on a pole over there near the dance circle," said Little Big Fat pointing in that direction.

"I heard that no one but the Medicine Man could touch that bag! Once someone tried to steal it and the medicine bundle sucked the blood right out of him!" said Little Voice Standing Small.

"Whoa...really?" asked Little Big Fat.

"Yes," answered Little Voice Standing Small as he and the boys continued to brew the black drink and watch the Medicine Man.

Just then, King Payne's two nephews joined them.

"Did you know that inside that medicine bundle is a powder that will put a man to sleep and a magical stone that will turn into a shield?" asked

Sitting Frog, one of the chief's nephews.

"Yes. There is also a horn from the underwater horned snake," added Blowing Wind, the chief's other nephew.

"What does the horn do?" asked Little Big Fat.

"It will help you hunt deer. The deer will come to you!" explained Sitting Frog.

"Wow! I would like to have that horn!" exclaimed Little Voice Standing Small who knew that was impossible.

"The medicine bundle also holds the fangs of a rattlesnake. The Medicine Man scratches warrior's arms and legs with them," explained Sitting Frog.

"Why?" asked Little Big Fat, thinking how that would hurt.

"It makes the warriors stronger!" answered Sitting Frog.

"Don't look now, but here comes the Medicine Man!" said Little Voice Standing Small. All the boys looked down at the pot and stirred madly. They were afraid of the magical powers of the Medicine Man.

"Boys, is the black drink boiling yet?' asked the Medicine Man.

"Yes," said the scared boys.

"Good, it is time for the men to take their first drink," said the Medicine Man as he motioned for the men to come forward.

The Seminole men drank the black drink quickly and then yelled "Asi-Yahola" before they got sick!

"Yuck! They are all throwing up, Little Voice Standing Small!" exclaimed Little Big Fat, who was looking rather sickly now himself.

"Don't look at them!" advised Little Voice Standing Small.

"Why do they drink it?" asked Little Big Fat.

"They drink it to clean out their bodies of any sickness," explained Sitting Frog.

Next, the men performed the "feather dance" using pretty white feathers. It was now noon and time for "court."

"Look, here comes the chief, King Payne, and his brother, Bowlegs," said Little Big Fat who was feeling much better now.

The most important Seminole leaders entered the Big House and sat down. The Medicine Man and all the Seminole warriors entered next. It was now time for "court."

The thief, whose name was "Lying on the Ground Creeping" was the last to enter the Big House. He hung his head in shame as he stood in front of his Seminole leaders.

"I stole from all of you...from your mothers, your brothers, and your sisters. I was not to be trusted," confessed Lying on the Ground Creeping.

"Yes," agreed the Medicine Man. "We fear you may take what is not yours again."

"I am sorry," said Lying on the Ground Creeping with tears in his eyes. "I will not trouble you again. I have shamed myself and my family. I welcome my punishment."

"Did you hear that?" whispered Little Big Fat who was sitting outside the Big House with the other boys listening to "court." "I can't believe he wants to be punished!"

"He knows if he isn't punished, he could be exiled!" explained Little Voice Standing Small quietly. "And then he could never return!"

The Medicine Man turned to the chief, King Payne to talk about the thief's punishment.

"Little Voice Standing Small, are you hungry?" asked Little Big Fat whose stomach was now growling from hunger.

"Shhh...those fasting are the one's who should be hungry. Not you!" answered Little Voice Standing Small. "Listen, the punishment has been decided."

The chief's speaker now answered the thief – Lying on the Ground Creeping. "Yes, you must be punished. You will work for the people you stole from. You will be their slave for 100 days!" He then handed Lying on the Ground Creeping a bag of 100 sticks. "Remove one stick for each day that you repay your sin. The day the last one is cast aside, will be the day, that we will forgive you!"

Other men now came forward and confessed their sins too. All were forgiven until next year's Green Corn Dance.

MEDICINE BUNDLE

Chapter VII - Say My Name, Say My Name, "Alligator"

That night the Medicine Man opened up the medicine bundle for all to see. The boys were the first to gather around the unlit campfire and watch. The Medicine Man carefully unwrapped all the pieces. Some items were too powerful to touch, so he used the wing bones of a buzzard to pick them up with.

"Is that the magical stone?" asked Little Big Fat who was enjoying eating a roasted squirrel.

"Yes," whispered Blowing Wind. "And there's the magic medicine called 'shot-in-the-heart.'"

"What is it used for?" asked Little Voice Standing Small.

"It's used to cure the warrriors' wounds," explained Sitting Frog.

"Look, that has to be the snake horn!" exclaimed Little Big Fat.

"Yes, and there are the bones of the 'little people' that live in the woods!" said Blowing Wind.

"DO NOT TOUCH ANYTHING!" warned the Medicine Man.

The startled boys jumped at his strong loud words. They were too afraid to touch anything. To them, it was as if, that medicine bundle was full of rattlesnakes!

The Medicine Man next held a rock above his head and exclaimed, "I will now light the medicine fire with this special piece of flint! Boys, bring me four ears of green corn."

Little Voice Standing Small, Little Big Fat, Sitting Frog, and Blowing Wind ran as fast as they could to get the green corn. They would always obey the Medicine Man. They

L.L. Eadie

were too afraid not too. They returned shortly, out of breath, with armfuls of green corn!

"Whoa, boys! Thank you, but all I needed were four ears of green corn!" laughed the Medicine Man. He placed one ear of corn to the north, one to the south, one east and one west around the sacred medicine fire. "Boys, it is now time to cook more black drink. It should boil till midnight," said the Medicine Man and then he turned and walked away.

"Yuck! Why do we have to cook the stinky black drink again?" asked Little Big Fat.

"Remember, tonight after midnight we will become men and that means that we will never have to cook the black drink ever again!" exclaimed Blowing Wind.

"But...then we will have to drink it!" laughed Little Voice Standing Small and the other boys laughed too as they stirred the smelly black drink.

At midnight the Medicine Man put four ears of roasted green corn into the black drink. The fasting men drank it and once again they became sick. However, soon they all were dancing the Green Corn Dance around the sacred medicine fire.

Little Voice Standing Small and the other boys sat as quiet as deer hidden in the woods. The men continued to dance in the smoke of the sacred medicine fire. The Medicine Man became a storyteller. He told tall tales to King Payne; the chief's brother, Bowlegs, and the chief's speaker. They were all listening to his stories. And the boys, had the eyes and the ears of a panther, that night, under the moon and stars.

"What are you thinking, Little Voice Standing Small?" whispered Little Big Fat as he sat next to him.

"I don't know. Lots of memories are flooding my head," answered Little Voice Standing Small.

"Are you thinking about the one-eyed alligator?" asked Little Big Fat.

"Yes, and about Gold, the little person I told you about. I wonder if I will ever see them again. What are you thinking about, Little Big Fat...food?" laughed Little Voice Standing Small quietly.

"No. I am thinking that I hope I never see your one-eyed alligator ever again. However, I sure would like to meet Gold though. Little Voice Standing Small, what do you think my new grown-up name will be?"

"Well, let's see...maybe... 'Smells Like Urine!'" laughed Little Voice Standing Small a little too loud.

At that moment the music, dancing, and storytelling stopped. Little Voice Standing Small's and Little Big Fat's uncles along with the other men from the Seminole bands approached the boys. Their time had finally arrived!

Little Big uncle escorted him up to the Medicine Man and announced his new name, "Hawk Eyes." Little Voice Standing Small thought that this was a great name for his good friend. After all, if it had not been for Little Big Fat's good sight, he would have been attacked by the alligator!

Now, it was Little Voice Standing Small's turn. "My nephew, Little Voice Standing Small is very brave...with one arrow he scared away a bull alligator! His new name is Alligator (Halpatter)," said his uncle proudly to the Medicine Man.

"Hello, Alligator. You are come," greeted the Medicine Man as they shook arms.

It was now Alligator's turn to feel proud. "My name is Alligator! My name is Alligator!" he said over and over to himself. And then, as if it was planned, the first dance was — the alligator!

Chapter VIII - The Green Corn Dance is Over, When the Fast is Broken

No one slept that night. The Seminoles stayed up with the owls in the woods. They danced like a screech owl, a woodpecker, a catfish, a horse, a chicken, and an alligator. When they weren't dancing, they were lending an ear to the Medicine Man's tall tales.

At dawn the stories had ended, and the Medicine Man carefully packed away the magical items into the medicine bundle. He then headed out alone into the forest to hide the medicine bundle in a secret place. When he returned the fast would be broken and a big breakfast would be eaten and enjoyed by everyone!

"Did you hear about the 'scratching?'" asked Little Big Fat at breakfast, whose new name was Hawk Eyes.

"Yes, I don't think it hurts...not any worse than a snake bite," teased Little Voice Standing Small, who was now called Alligator.

"No, it's just a little needle, Hawk Eyes," added Pond Governor, Sitting Frog's new grown-up name.

"Yes, he just pricks you with it. It doesn't really hurt," explained Long Tom, the new name for Blowing Wind.

"Why do we have to be 'scratched?'" asked the worried Hawk Eyes.

"To clean your blood...you don't want to be sick, do you?" answered Pond Governor.

"No!" exclaimed everyone.

After breakfast the Medicine Man stuck all the Seminole men with the needle. Their dirty blood, that would have made them sick, dribbled out onto the ground. The men would now be well for another year.

It was now time to pack up and head home. The Green Corn Dance was over for this year. Alligator could not remember a better time in his entire life! His future, and his friend's future, looked promising. They all *should have* lived happily ever after. However, instead, the white man like the twins—thunder and lightning—struck the Seminoles!

Chapter IX - Friends Revisited

The sky above was full of stars as the Seminole Indians returned to their villages from the Green Corn Dance. Sleep was not far away. As soon as their bags were lightened, their eyes were heavy and closed.

"So, your name is Alligator, now, huh?" asked the little person, Gold, as he sat on the chest of the sleeping Seminole Indian, Alligator, formerly called Little Voice Standing Small.

"What? Who is it?" asked Alligator startled awake.

"It's me, Gold! Your good luck charm! Remember I helped you pull the arrow out of the one-eyed alligator's blind eye. I've come for my handful of gold beads you promised.

"Mmmm...as I recall it, Gold, you ran away," said Alligator as he lifted Gold from his chest and sat up in his hammock.

"I was there! I saw you remove the arrow! I protected you from the one-eyed alligator! If it was not for me, *you* would be known as the One-Armed Alligator!" exclaimed Gold who was now sitting next to him grinning.

"Okay, okay, the gold beads are yours," laughed Alligator. He then handed Gold a small buckskin bag of gold beads from his belt sash.

The next morning when Alligator woke up, he wondered if he had dreamed the whole thing.

"Mother, did you see the little person here last night?"

"No. Was he here? What did he want?"

"I'm not sure...maybe...let's see..." Alligator felt his belt sash for his gold beads. They were missing. "I guess he really was here. I gave him his reward."

"I wish I had met him," said Alligator's mother. "Well, Little Voice Standing Small, oops...I mean Alligator, what are your plans on your first day of manhood? I know it's not collecting firewood."

"No, Uncle is taking me deer hunting," said Alligator proudly.

"And alligator hunting too," added his uncle as he entered their hut.

"Hello, Uncle, I am ready!" said the excited Alligator.

That evening after a long day's hunt, as the sun set, Alligator and his uncle set out in a canoe on the big lake by their village to hunt alligators. "You did well today, Alligator," said his uncle as he poled the canoe in the shallow water. He next pinched his nose and grunted like an alligator, to call one.

"But...I missed the deer, Uncle," said Alligator, who was disappointed.

"Don't worry. How many stars do you see in the sky?"

"I don't know. Too many to count," answered Alligator as he lifted his face to the now starlit sky.

"Yes, and that is how many deer, black bear, fish, and other game there are on our Seminole lands. You will have many chances," said his uncle smiling.

"I will try not to disappoint you tonight, Uncle."

"Fire the torch for me, Alligator! I see one!"

Alligator's uncle held the lit torch as Alligator stood in the canoe aiming his uncle's firearm at the alligator floating on the water. He closed one eye as he aimed. Alligator did not want to disappoint his uncle again. He must shoot this alligator! The canoe drifted closer to the alligator and *his eye* shined in the dark like a star. This alligator had only one shining eye!

"No! I'm sorry, Uncle, but I cannot shoot *this* alligator!" exclaimed Alligator as he lowered his uncle's firearm. The one-eyed alligator disappeared under the dark water.

"That was him, wasn't it?" asked his uncle who now lowered the fiery torch.

"Yes. Are you disappointed in me, Uncle?"

"No. I am proud to see your respect for your one-eyed alligator. And he will not forget it either!"

Historical Summary - The Green Corn Dance -
"What's in A Name?"

Alligator's family belonged to the Lower Creek Indian tribe of Georgia. He was born in Georgia in 1795. His tribe migrated to Florida in search of game. They became part of the Alachua Seminole band. Alligator and around sixty to seventy Seminoles lived along the northeast side of Alligator Lake in present day Lake City, Florida, formerly called Alligator Town (Halpata Tolophka) up until 1859. Today there is a park named in Alligator Warrior's honor on the north side of Alligator Lake. It is most appropriately named "Halpatter Park."

In Florida, the Creek tribe became known as the Seminoles during the 1770's. The Spanish called them "cimmarones" or "free people." The U.S. citizens called them the Seminoles. Later the meaning of the word changed to "wild people" or "runaways." The Florida Seminole prefer "unconquered people." Other tribes that joined the Seminoles were the Yamassee, Yuchi, Tequesta, Appalachicola, Choctaw, and Oconee along with escaped and freed African slaves known as Maroons or Afro-Seminoles. Some the the early Seminole Indians did possess African slaves; however, they were virtually free. Their slaves paid a tithe to their Seminole chief for protection – often part of their harvest. Some Maroons either married or were adopted by the Seminoles and other Maroons formed their own bands and had their own leaders.

Part One is a fictional account of how Alligator Warrior might have received his adult Seminole name. I chose his childhood name of Little Voice Standing Small because Seminole children were known to play quietly, and secondly because Alligator was short (5') in comparison to other Seminole men (6'). Seminole children's names are traditionally connected to a meaningful experience. When

37

boys reached adulthood (13 – 15 years old) they received a new name during the Green Corn Dance. (Girls kept their childhood names.) No two boys were given the same name. Sometimes men were even given another name for a special achievement, like an act of bravery. Alligator later earned the name "Warrior" (Tustennuggee). It was the highest class of a warrior and he was considered then a sub-chief or war chief. White men sometime gave the Indians other names as well, because their Seminole names were too difficult for them to pronounce.

The Green Corn Dance lasted four days and was the occasion for a yearly purification, forgiveness, and rejoicing. It took place anywhere from April to mid July. The Seminoles referred to this time as the "little moon in June." Each Indian village received fifteen sticks as a way to give notice of the upcoming Green Corn Dance. Each day a stick was removed. The day the last stick was removed signaled the villages to travel to the chosen place for the celebration.

Some of the Green Corn Dance rituals were playing games such as "Little Brother of War" – a competition between Seminole towns that was played on a field with goals at either end and another game played with a wooden bat and a stuffed deerskin ball. The aim of the game was to hit the tree with the ball. Other players could push, shove and block your attempt.

The terribly smelly bitter tasting black drink was drunk to cleanse the body and the "scratching" was to ensure good health both instructed and performed by the medicine man. His medicine bundle's appearance was an entire deerskin complete with the head of a buck. It held hundreds of objects all wrapped in animal skins. The Seminoles believed if the bundle was not handled carefully it could bring harm to the entire group; causing great pain in their heads and joints and the loss of their bodies' blood. It was hidden by the medicine man and no other Indian knew its whereabouts. Presently there are eight medicine bundles in Florida. Medicine men still guard them.

Another Green Corn Dance ritual was the dances, old man's dance and steal-a-partner dance. Most dances were in honor of a specific animal: catfish dance, chicken dance, quail dance, screech owl dance, woodpecker dance, alligator dance, and other dances named after Florida wildlife.

The Seminole Indians have a rich culture of customs and beliefs. To greet one another they shook arms, not hands, and said, "You are come" instead of "Nice to meet you." Their children were raised by their mothers' family. Sons were taught by their uncles instead of their fathers. Their father provided for them but was not part of their children's clan. Clan membership was inherited through the mother. It was a matrilineal society. Another Seminole belief was that if twins were born, they had to be separated because they would cause too much havoc together. They were compared to thunder and lightning.

Seminoles also believed that "reality could transcend ordinary existence." In other words, they believed that an animal could speak, or a rock could move. They believed in "little people" or little human-like dwarf creatures, similar to leprechauns that existed in either trees or good luck charms, especially for hunting. However, the Seminoles were cautious of them. The little people were mischievous, naughty, and playful. They were considered good luck charms, especially for hunting. A Seminole legend said that thunder and lightning tried to kill the little people, who often times lived in the holes of the oldest trees. They believed that is why lightning strikes trees.

Another Seminole legendard mythical creature was the serpent. He could be very large or very small. The serpent had unusual abilities. It was believed that he lived in the wetlands and swamps of Florida. He could sometimes help the Indians by bringing them good fortune or protect them from harm. The Seminoles' serpent was called the "Dragon Snake." It commonly lived in Lake Okeechobee. Another myth of the Seminoles was that an alligator would bite you if you made fun of it and another was that a rabbit was always portrayed as a trickster and a liar...just like Brer Rabbit or Bugs Bunny today.

The Seminoles did not live in tepees, but rather huts similar to log cabins. Later when they moved south of Ocala, they built homes without exterior walls called "chickees." Chickees were very practical for the hot, humid and wet Florida climate. It had a thatched palmetto roof on an above ground wood floor. The floor was raised for their protection from their environment.

The Seminole Indian fire used entire logs. One end of the log was pushed into the fire and consumed while the other end extended out. A big community pot of food was hung over the fire. A favorite was "coontie" bread that was made from a wild potato. Another staple food was "sofkee" made from ground corn and similar to grits.

The Seminoles dressed in garments of bright colored fabrics, turbans and moccasins. Seminole men wore several handkerchiefs tied around their necks. Their turban exposed the top of the man's head. Often one or two plumes from egrets, herons, osprey, or wild turkeys adorned their turbans. Seminoles never wore a feather from the powerful eagle as western Indians did. Seminole women wore beads around their necks, usually blue stones. The women also enjoyed wearing silver disks necklaces, earrings and large rings. Men also wore silver engraved crescent shaped disks called "gorgets" on necklaces.

King Payne was the Seminole Indian chief from 1784 – 1812. He reigned from Payne's Prairie near present-day Gainesville, Florida. King Payne inherited his chieftain from his uncle (his mother's brother), Cowkeeper. He was also known as Seacoffee. Cowkeeper was called this because of his huge cattle herds; formerly belonging to the Spanish. Early Muskogee Seminoles were known as the "Cow Creek Seminoles." King Payne also had a sister whose two sons were named Long Tom and Pond Governor. Pond Governor later became Chief Micanopy. His sister had two daughters. One married King Philip. This couple's son became the famous "Coacoochee" or better known as "Wildcat." Wildcat and Alligator became leaders during the Second Seminole War along with others including Osceola.

Part II - The First Seminole War: "The White Patriots Verses the Red Patriots"

Chapter I - Indian Giver

Four Green Corn Dances later, the Seminoles were no longer alone on their land. There were now new settlers. These strangers were white men from Georgia. They took what did not belong to them. These white settlers never said "sorry" or "thank you" to the Indians. King Payne became worried and called a council meeting. All the Seminole men across north Florida attended.

"We will leave for Payne's Town with the next rising sun," said Alligator's uncle to the men of their village. All the men, both young and old gathered together by the shore of the big lake. Alligator could tell that his uncle was worried.

"Uncle," said Alligator.

"Yes?" answered his uncle.

"Do these white men have good or bad souls?" asked Alligator.

"We are not sure. They seem not to respect *us* or *our land*. They could be our enemy. I want you, Alligator, to travel to the Seminole Maroon village today and tell them about the council meeting. You may ride my horse, Black Thunder. He is much faster than your pony," explained his uncle.

Alligator smiled. His uncle's horse, Black Thunder, was the fastest Indian horse. He was also the biggest and most beautiful black horse in the whole village. However, Black Thunder would not allow anyone else but his uncle to ride him!

"Don't worry, Alligator. I will speak to him," said his uncle.

Alligator watched quietly as his uncle whispered into Black Thunder's ear. Black Thunder turned his head and looked at Alligator. He nodded his head as if he understood.

"Thank you," said Alligator as he climbed up onto the back of Black Thunder. Alligator felt very grown-up and proud. He galloped off like the wind towards the Maroon village. This was a very important task his uncle had given him. Alligator would make sure he did not disappoint him!

Alligator had ridden for about an hour when he saw two white men in the distance. The white men did not see him. Alligator remembered what his uncle had said about these men, *"They could be our enemy!"* He climbed down off Black Thunder's back and led the horse behind some tall thick bushes along the dirt roadside.

"Shhh...Black Thunder," whispered Alligator as he rubbed the horse's head to calm him. Black Thunder again seemed to understand and nodded his head.

The white men did not see Alligator and Black Thunder hiding in the bushes. They walked right past them. To Alligator's surprise, the white men were not alone. Walking behind them in chains was Moses! These white men were slave catchers! Alligator thought to himself, "Moses is no longer a slave. He is a proud Seminole Maroon Indian!" Alligator suddenly had a plan and whispered it into Black Thunder's ear. Once again Black Thunder nodded his head to show that he understood. Slowly, so very slowly Alligator climbed back up onto Black Thunder's back. They had to be very quiet so that the slave catchers wouldn't hear them. Black Thunder did not charge out of the bushes but walked very slowly, just as Alligator had told him. Not only was Black Thunder the fastest Seminole horse but also the smartest thought Alligator.

"Hello there, I see you caught a runaway slave. He does not look like a very good one to me. He looks dirty and weak," said Alligator pretending not to know Moses.

Moses smiled at Alligator but did not speak his name. Alligator was his first Seminole friend. He had saved Moses and his family and now Alligator was here to save him again!

The two white men were very surprised to see this Seminole Indian. He seemed to appear out of the clear blue sky! "Who, who, who...where, where, where...what, what, what...?" stuttered the slave catchers.

"My name is Alligator and I am looking for a slave too...for myself. Can we trade? I'll trade you this fine big strong horse of mine for your little weak slave boy."

The two men whispered to each other. This was a very tempting trade for them. The horse was beautiful and could bring them a lot more money than this little boy.

"Okay, it's a deal!" said one of the slave catchers as the other one unchained Moses.

Alligator climbed down off Black Thunder. Moses quickly walked over to Alligator and whispered, "Are you sure about this?"

"Yes," said Alligator as he smiled and whispered into Moses' ear, "Do as I do."

It happened just as Alligator planned. As soon as the two white men climbed up onto Black Thunder's back, he threw them off and galloped over to Alligator and Moses! Alligator and Moses quickly jumped up on Black Thunder's back and were gone before the slave catchers could brush the dirt off the seat of their pants!

"You, Indian giver!" laughed Moses as they rode off to his Maroon village.

Chapter II - The Garden of King Payne's Eden

S ummer still lay thick in the air as the Seminole men and their families set out for Payne's Town. Beautiful wildflowers and grapevines seemed to follow them down the sandy road. Big blooms on the magnolia trees fragranced the warm sticky air. Spanish moss swayed in the light breeze as it hung from the branches of most trees. As the Indians approached Payne's Town, they could see blankets and old clothes hanging in the trees to scare away the crows from the Seminole gardens. The young boys could be heard whooping in the corn fields as they chased away the "stealers of the corn," the crows. There were herds of cows, sheep, goats, and horses in the big prairie. In the distance they could see the big two-story home of King Payne.

"Look, Alligator and Hawk Eyes, there's the Big Jug (Alachua)," said Alligator's uncle pointing in the direction of a water-filled sinkhole.

"Why do they call it the Big Jug?" asked Alligator as he rode his pony next to his uncle, who rode the mighty Black Thunder.

"They call the Big Jug that because it is bottomless! There is not enough water to fall from the sky to fill it!" answered his uncle.

"There could be a scary serpent living in there!" exclaimed Hawk Eyes.

"Maybe, but most serpents live in the Big Lake (Okeechobee)," said Alligator's uncle.

"I have never seen a serpent...have you uncle?" asked Alligator.

"No," answered his uncle shaking his head.

"What do they look like? Does anyone know?" asked Hawk Eyes as he looked at the Big Jug.

"Many who have seen the serpent call him the "Dragon Snake." This is because he looks like the biggest snake you will ever see!" explained Alligator's uncle.

Just at that moment Hawk Eyes spotted King Payne in the distance. "There's King Payne!" exclaimed Hawk Eyes who was happy to change the subject. He was scared of the thought of a "Dragon Snake!"

"King Payne rode out to meet his guests on his beautiful white horse. He looked very regal. His hair was now white as his horse's. King Payne was eighty years old.

"Hello. You are come," said King Payne as he shook their arms to greet them. "Follow me to the house. There is a delicious feast waiting for you and all of my Seminole bands."

This was good news to the tired and hungry Indians. Many had traveled for several days. It was the best news Hawk Eyes had heard! He was starving!

"Wow, did you hear that, Alligator? A feast!" said the excited and always hungry Hawk Eyes.

"Yes, it's a good thing King Payne has big herds of animals and fields of corn!" laughed Alligator teasing his hungry friend.

There was plenty of food for all. The roasted meats were Hawk Eyes' favorite. He wrapped some up in his scarf for a snack later.

"Just look at King Payne's house!" exclaimed Alligator as he walked in the front door with Hawk Eyes. He had never been in such a grand house.

"It looks just like my old master's plantation house," said Moses as he joined Alligator and Hawk Eyes by the pretty staircase.

"Yes, the Spanish have given King Payne many white man gifts," agreed Alligator looking around at the furniture, vases and pictures on the walls.

"That is because the Spanish fear him!" exclaimed Moses who was very proud to be a Seminole Maroon Indian and no longer a slave.

Alligator smiled and said, "Yes, but they also give him gifts because he is a good chief!"

"I was looking for you two. I have a good idea...tonight after the council fire at midnight...let's go serpent hunting!" suggested Moses who had heard the Dragon Snake stories from his new family of Maroon Indians.

"No way, not me!" exclaimed Hawk Eyes.

"We need your hawk eyes for spotting the Dragon Snake," encouraged Alligator who thought this serpent hunting sounded like fun.

"Yes," agreed Moses nodding his head and smiling.

"Okay," said the unsure Hawk Eyes who thought this Dragon Snake hunting sounded very scary.

That evening at midnight as the wings of the owl flapped and the deer slept soundly in the woods, the Seminole men gathered around the council fire. A large gourd filled with the bad tasting black drink and tobacco filled pipes were passed around to all the men. Everyone both young and old smoked the pipe and drank the black drink, including Alligator and Hawk Eyes.

"The clouds are lowering over our heads and the land is shrinking under our feet. We are the proud Seminoles. We are free to roam and hunt. We must keep it that way! Peace! We must make peace with this new white man settler," declared King Payne who was the first to speak.

"Yes," agreed most of the Seminole men nodding their heads.

"I agree brother, but these palefaces have a forked tongue. They make white lies and say they are our friends but then they steal our cattle, our land and our slaves!" explained Bowlegs, King Payne's brother.

"Yes," agreed most of the Seminole men again.

"We must not take what is not ours either. I have been told that we also have taken cattle from the white man. And they believe we steal their slaves too," said King Payne.

"No! Again, their tongues are forked. They bite the hand they shake!" answered Bowlegs.

"We must return to the white man his cattle and his slaves. We must make peace with the white man! Listen to me; there are many more white men than Seminoles. We must take care of our families. Our earth is made of glass right now. We must be careful not to break it! Peace!" exclaimed King Payne.

"PEACE!" exclaimed everyone and then the dancing began around the council fire.

49

Chapter III - The Big Jug's (Alachua's) Dragon Snake

A s dawn broke the council men headed to their cabins for sleep but Alligator, Hawk Eyes and Moses walked down the sandy road to the Big Jug (Alachua). There was no breeze this morning, so the Spanish moss hung still in the tall trees that lined the narrow road. The early birds were singing and seeking food in the prairie where the herds of cows, goats and sheep quietly grazed. They animals paid no attention to the three young Seminoles.

"Why did I let you two talk me into this?" asked the worried Hawk Eyes as they walked in the cool morning sand.

"Don't you want to see the scary Dragon Snake?" asked Moses laughing.

"No!" said Hawk Eyes.

"We told you, Hawk Eyes, we need your hawk eyes for spotting the serpent!" laughed Alligator. Even though Moses and Alligator teased Hawk Eyes they really did need him and were just as scared as he was.

"I don't believe either one of you!" laughed Hawk Eyes too.

"I think it would be a good idea if we took the Dragon Snake a friendship offering," suggested Moses.

"Good idea, Moses! We'll give the serpent, Hawk Eyes, as a sacrifice offering!" joked Alligator laughing again.

"Very funny," laughed Hawk Eyes. He knew his friends were only teasing him.

"Now we don't want to make the Dragon Snake mad...*do we?* We should give him a *good* present!" said Moses laughing.

"What about gold beads?" asked Gold, the little person, who suddenly appeared and surprised them.

"GOLD! Hello! You are come!" greeted Alligator. "Meet my friends, Hawk Eyes and Moses."

"Hello friends of Alligator. So, it's the Dragon Snake you are seeking this time. What is it with you, Alligator? You are always looking for trouble!" said Gold smiling.

"Yes, you are right my little good luck charm. Hawk Eyes and Moses, good news, Gold will protect us!" explained Alligator.

"Have you ever seen the serpent, Gold?" asked Hawk Eyes who was feeling much better now that Gold, Alligator's good luck charm, had showed up.

"*Have I ever seen the Dragon Snake*? Does King Payne ride a white horse? Does the medicine bundle hold magical things? Does the black drink taste bad? Well, of course, I've seen the Dragon Snake!" exclaimed Gold waving his short arms up and down.

"What does the serpent look like?" asked Alligator.

"Let's see..." said Gold as he rubbed his little chin. "He has a very long body with yellow and brown diamond shapes on his back and a horn on his head and ..."

"Does he have big teeth?" interrupted Hawk Eyes.

"I don't know," answered Gold shrugging his small shoulders.

"*You don't know*?" asked the alarmed Hawk Eyes who now was worried that Gold had lied like a rabbit and that he had never really seen the Dragon Snake before!

"Yes, that's what I said! I know you can see so is something wrong with your hearing?" asked Gold shaking his small head madly. Gold was angry because he was being questioned.

51

"Well, let's go find out!" said Alligator smiling and patting Hawk Eyes on the back and Gold on top of the head. He knew better than to make a little person mad!

"Hold on! Not so fast! We haven't talked about what I get for protecting you from the serpent!" exclaimed Gold.

"Well, I don't have anymore gold beads," said Alligator.

"Well, good luck then," said Gold as he turned and began walking away.

"WAIT! Don't go! I have some roasted meat from King Payne's feast. It's delicious!" said Hawk Eyes as he showed Gold the meat tied up in his neck scarf.

"Are you for real? Do you really think I want to eat your old meat you've had your dirty fingers all over?" asked Gold as he kept walking.

"STOP! I have some gold!" exclaimed Moses as he removed his gold earring from his ear. The earring was a gift from his new Seminole Maroon father.

"Mmmm...let me see it!" said Gold as he walked back and took the earring from Moses. He bit it to see if it was really gold. "Okay, it's a deal, I'll go."

"Moses, you keep your earring. I'll get you some gold...some how. Don't worry Gold, you know you can trust me," said Alligator. Alligator didn't want his friend, Moses, to give away his special gift.

"Well...okay," agreed Gold.

The Big Jug's water sparkled like gold in the morning sun as they cast a canoe off the sandy shore. There was no wind to stir ripples on the top of the water. Moses and Alligator paddled the canoe while Hawk Eyes sat up front looking for the serpent. Gold once again climbed up onto Alligator's shoulder to sit.

"I see something...it's...it's...over there!" exclaimed Hawk Eyes pointing at a dark object floating in the still water.

All at once the canoe began shaking!

"What is it?" asked Moses who now was really scared too. Gold was so frightened that he climbed down and hid on the floor of the canoe.

"It's you two! The two of you are shaking so hard, you're rocking the boat!" laughed Alligator. "It's only an old log floating over there!"

Gold peeked over the canoe's side to make sure. He then climbed back up on Alligator's shoulder. "I must have fallen off your shoulder when they rocked the canoe," lied Gold.

Moses and Hawk Eyes started laughing at Gold *and* at each other. "Some lucky charm you are!" laughed Moses.

"Whew, that was a close one! I really thought we had found the Dragon Snake!" confessed Hawk Eyes laughing.

"Me, too!" laughed Moses.

All at once the water in the Big Jug began to boil! Their canoe began to spin in circles!

"WHAT'S HAPPENING?" shouted Moses and Hawk Eyes as they held onto the sides of the swirling canoe. Alligator held on tight too! Gold tried hopping off Alligator's shoulder into the canoe once more but instead fell overboard into the stirred-up water!

"GOLD! GOLD!" shouted Alligator looking over the canoe's side for his little friend. However, Gold was gone! Alligator jumped into the boiling water to save Gold! Alligator was now gone too! Hawk Eyes and Moses began to cry.

Several moments later the Dragon Snake surfaced! Gold was telling the truth he did have a long body with yellow and brown diamonds on his back and a horn on his head. But he also had two humps on his back. And riding safely on one, was Alligator and on the other hump was Gold!

"Hello, Moses and Hawk Eyes! Look who we found in the Big Jug!" exclaimed Alligator waving and smiling at his friends along with Gold, as they rode the serpent's humps up and down. When Alligator's hump went up, Gold's went down...and when Gold's went up, Alligator's went down.

"Would you like to go for a ride too?" asked the friendly serpent as he circled the canoe smiling showing his two long teeth.

"Would you like some roasted meat?" asked Hawk Eyes as he held out the meat in his shaking hand as a friendship offering.

"Why yes, thank you," said the Dragon Snake and then he surprised Hawk Eyes by sticking out his very long pink tongue and licking the meat right out of Hawk Eyes' shaking hand. However, not only did he lick Hawk Eyes' hand, but also his whole face! Everyone laughed including Hawk Eyes.

"What is your name?" asked Moses as he climbed onto one of the humps as Alligator and Gold moved to the canoe.

"I have no name," said the serpent shaking his long neck slowly back and forth.

"What did your mother call you?" asked Hawk Eyes who held on tightly to the other hump waiting for their ride around the Big Jug.

"I have no mother," answered the Dragon Snake sadly as he swam slowly across the now still water with Hawk Eyes and Moses on his back.

"Family?" asked Alligator from the canoe where Gold now rested on his shoulder again.

"No," answered the serpent shaking his long neck again.

"Friends?" asked Gold.

"No one wants to be my friend. I am a monster. Everyone is afraid of me," said the Dragon Snake sadly. "Are you all afraid of me?"

54

"No!" exclaimed everyone.

"Then will all of you be my friend?" asked the Dragon Snake.

"Yes!" exclaimed everyone.

"My name is Alligator, and this is the little person called Gold. And riding on your back is my fellowhood brother, Hawk Eyes. And Moses, the one who leads his family tribe out of slavery, is on your other hump. We all want to be your friend!" exclaimed Alligator proudly and everyone nodded their heads and smiled.

"Thank you! You may call me...well... let's see...my name will be...FRIEND (Uh-hiss-see)!" said the smiling Dragon Snake showing his two long teeth again. Hawk Eyes was sure glad this serpent had chosen 'Friend' as his name!

Chapter IV - Hard Rain Falls on Paradise

Just like the surprise meeting with the serpent, the white men's attack came as a surprise too! The white men wanted the Seminole's paradise. They would not stop until they got it. Tears fell from the sky when King Payne died.

"No! Tell me it is not so! Wake me and tell me it's just a nightmare of darkness. Oh, Great Spirit (Pohyyah), take my brothers into the Hereafter," cried Alligator as he stood alone on the sandy shore of the big lake. His eyes stared without looking across its still waters. The lake did not seem to see his sadness, but then the tree frogs began to croak and thus a hard rain began to fall, and the lake cried too.

"Yes, I wish too that it was just a bad dream, but *my eye* does not lie," said the one-eyed alligator who suddenly surfaced. The hard rain seemed to dance on his back in the crying lake. "Many more white men will come, Alligator. Your battle for your Seminole paradise has only just begun!"

"You know then, one-eyed alligator, that many Seminole warriors' spirits have left with the wind and gone to the happy hunting grounds? My uncle, who was like a father to me...and now the great King Payne has left us too! Why?" asked Alligator sadly.

The one-eyed alligator had no answer for him, so he said nothing. The hard rain continued to fall on them and their paradise...and they cried too.

"You know, Alligator, you will see them again," said the one-eyed alligator.

"Of course, you are right. Thank you," answered Alligator who was now smiling at the wise words of the one-eyed alligator. The sun smiled too, and the hard rain stopped. A beautiful rainbow stretched across the sky.

"Your time has come, Alligator. Your uncle taught you well. You will soon become a great warrior (tustenuggee)!" And with those final words the one-eyed alligator disappeared under the tea-colored waters of the big lake by Alligator's village.

The war King Payne had warned the Seminoles about had begun. The white man, Colonel Newnan, had taken the life of their peaceful leader King Payne and fifty other Seminole warriors including Alligator's uncle. Bowlegs, King Payne's brother, was now the Seminoles' chief.

Bowlegs told the sad Seminoles, "We must prepare our loved ones for their journey to the Hereafter. The Great Spirit awaits them. Dress them in new clothes. Paint a red spot on their right cheek and a black one on their left. In their left hand place a piece of burnt wood and in their right hand put a bow and arrow. Gather their valuables and break them before you place them in their grave."

Alligator and the other Seminole men carried the dead warriors to their graves as their sad families followed. Their mothers, sisters and daughters cried.

"We will mourn our fallen warriors for four moons. Go home now," said Chief Bowlegs at the Seminoles' funeral on the hill.

Alligator, Hawk Eyes, Pond Governor, and Long Tom stayed and guarded the warriors' graves. They made funeral fires to keep away the bad birds of the night.

"Do you think other white men will come, Alligator?" asked Pond Governor, as they sat by the funeral fires.

"Yes, the one-eyed alligator told me the war has only just begun. Many more white men will come. They will not leave until our paradise is *their* paradise!" answered Alligator. He hoped one day that he would become a warrior and help the Seminoles rid Florida, the village of many Indians, from their land.

"Is there not anything that we can do to stop them?' asked Hawk Eyes, who was looking to the sky for the bad birds. He was feeling rather scared as darkness fell like leaves from the trees around them.

"No. King Payne tried and now he is gone to the Happy Hunting Grounds...and so is my uncle," said Alligator as he added more firewood to the funeral fires.

"Bowlegs is our chief now! He will be able to stop the palefaces!" declared Long Tom.

"I hope so! But what if he can't? We must be ready to fight, or we too will be on *our* way too to the Happy Hunting Grounds!" exclaimed Alligator.

Chapter V - Crushing Spirit

Four hundred horsemen galloped towards the Seminole land. They had been ordered to loot and burn any Indian village they could find, steal their cattle and capture former slaves. Any Maroon found with a gun was to be shot and killed! No mercy! These white men were called volunteers. They carried their own guns. The Seminole booty would be their reward.

"King Payne spoke the truth. There are too many white men. Dark clouds continue to lower over our heads. Gather your families and whatever you can carry and leave your homes. Don't speak the word 'good-bye.' This is our land and we will return like the migrating bird after this season of darkness. I have heard the crying dog in the stillness of the dawn. He cries to warn us of more bad things to come!" said Chief Bowlegs to his Seminole warrior council.

"Yes," agreed the warriors nodding their heads. They also had heard the crying dog.

"Where will we go?" asked Long Tom.

"We will squirrel away our families down by the river. We will stand guard like a mother black bear over her cubs," declared Chief Bowlegs.

"Yes," agreed all the Seminole warriors again. The Seminole councilmen returned home to tell their families.

"My heart is heavy," cried Alligator's mother as she packed to leave their log hut by the big lake.

"Do not cry about leaving home, mother," said Alligator as he helped her pack.

"No, I cry for you, Alligator. I am old and have lived a good life. You, my son, are a young man and at the dawn of your life.

"Yes, I see...you fear for my life. I give you my word, mother; they will not hunt me down like an animal.

The volunteer horsemen came and found the Seminole villages abandoned. They burned the Indians' corn fields and homes. They stole their horses and cows. The white men destroyed everything! Now they searched for the Seminoles!

"They are coming! I see them!" whispered Hawk Eyes to the other warriors hiding in the swamp.

The Seminole warriors hid behind moss covered trees and bushes on small islands in the swamp. Big white birds flew over their heads and alligators and snakes swam close by. *And* so did the one-eyed alligator.

"Don't worry Alligator. These white men will not wade into the swamp. They are too afraid," said the one-eyed alligator that was floating in the dark waters within reach of Alligator.

"Yes. I believe you. We are safe and so are our families," said Alligator who hid behind a bush holding on tight to his dead uncle's rifle.

The white men's bullets fired into the swamp and shot over the Indians' heads, by their arms, legs, and sometimes wounded them. But still the white men stayed out of the swamp. The Seminoles fired back into the edge of night.

"I don't see them. I think they are gone," said Hawk Eyes as he peeked around a tall tree.

"They won't fight at night," said the one-eyed alligator as he swam away into the darkness of the still swamp.

"The one-eyed alligator is right. I will not forget his wise words. One day, I will surprise the white man and attack him at night," said Alligator.

"Yes, we must attack the palefaces like a wildcat pounces on a rabbit ...silently!" exclaimed Chief Bowlegs, who heard Alligator's words.

When the Seminoles returned to their villages, they found their homes and fields were made of ash! Their life in paradise was quickly fading into memories. They would return to the swamp, a place of soft sand and black water and the home of the alligators, snakes and now the Seminoles.

Chapter VI - The Alligator Horseman

Many seasons had come and gone when Pond Governor became the chief of the Seminole Indians. His new chief name was Micanopy. His town was called Cuscowilla.

"I like it here in Cuscowilla. Maybe Chief Micanopy has found a peaceful place for us to live," said Hawk Eyes as he stood on the sandy shore of the round lake by their new Indian village.

"Yes, it is guarded on one side by a swamp and the other side by a big forest," said Alligator pointing across the lake.

"I found some orange trees in that forest. The oranges are almost ripe and ready to pick and roast!" said Moses who was fishing on the bank nearby.

"Good! I am tired of eating palmetto cabbage," said Hawk Eyes.

"Me, too! It's too bad we can't grow much corn here. But it's just too wet," said Moses.

"And it's too bad we lost almost all of our cattle to the white men! All we have left are some skinny cows, pigs and chickens. If we didn't keep them tied up, we would not even have them!" exclaimed Hawk Eyes.

"I am afraid that there are hardly any skinny animals even left. They are hungry too," explained Alligator.

"Well, the fish don't seem to be too hungry. Or else the rabbit heard me say I was going fishing and told the fish not to bite!" laughed Moses as he began pulling his fishing line out of the water. All at once his pole bent!

"You've caught something!" shouted Hawk Eyes as he pointed with excitement at Moses' bent fishing pole.

"Pull harder!" shouted Alligator.

Moses pulled as hard as he could. His feet began to sink into the wet sand on the bank.

"There it is! I see it! It's...it's...it's an alligator skull!" laughed Hawk Eyes.

Alligator walked into the shallow water full of tall grass and picked up the skull. "I like it! May I have it, Moses?" asked Alligator.

"Yes. I don't want it, it's yours!" said Moses smiling at his good friend.

"Thank you. I'm sure I will find a good use for it. Would you like to join me and Hawk Eyes' hunting party this morning, Moses?" asked Alligator.

"What animal are you two hunting for?" asked Moses.

"Whatever game we can find," said Hawk Eyes rubbing his growling stomach.

"Everyone is very hungry. There are many mouths to feed. I am sure they would not even care if we brought back an ugly possum for dinner!" laughed Alligator.

"But aren't you afraid of the white men? They may catch us!" asked Moses.

"This is still our land! We have to feed our families if we are going to survive!" explained Alligator.

The three brave Indians headed into the thick forest. Alligator carried his dead uncle's rifle and rode his beautiful horse, Black Thunder. Moses and Hawk Eyes walked ten steps behind Alligator carrying their bow and arrows. Their steps hardly made a sound as they walked on rocks, sticks, and thorny plants. Even their words were kept to a whisper.

"I am going to ride ahead and make sure there are no white men around," said Alligator quietly. It was not long before he and Black Thunder were out of sight in the thick woods.

"He is the bravest Seminole I know!" declared Moses.

"I agree. I am proud that he is my fellowhood brother," said Hawk Eyes.

All at once there was a 'mooing' noise in the distance. Both Indians stopped in their tracks and listened.

"There...over there! It's a cow! Moses, it's a cow! Oh boy, we are not going to go hungry tonight!" exclaimed Hawk Eyes as he pointed and ran in the direction of the mooing cow. Moses ran behind him. They were both laughing loudly. In their excitement they forgot about being quiet.

"Where do you think the cow came from?" asked Moses later as he and Hawk Eyes made a rope to tie around the cow's neck after they had found him.

"I don't know. But he belongs to us now!" laughed Hawk Eyes who could already smell the steaks cooking over their campfire tonight!

"Yes! Alligator will be so surprised!" exclaimed Moses proudly.

"And so should *you*!" said a strange man's voice.

Hawk Eyes and Moses turned around quickly and there he was...the white man!

The white man held a rifle in one hand and a bull whip in the other. Hawk Eyes and Moses were caught, and they were scared!

"Savages lay down your bow and arrows and take off your buckskin shirts! You, slave, hug that tree! And, you, Injun', hug that tree over there!" shouted the mean white man.

Hawk Eyes and Moses did what the white man said. They stood three feet apart with their arms wrapped around each tree. The white man used the same rope that they had just made, to tie their wrists together. Now, they could not escape.

"This is for rustling my cow!" shouted the angry white man as he lashed their bare backs one at a time. The pain was great, but Hawk Eyes and Moses did not cry out.

The white man did not hear *or see* Alligator as he quietly approached him atop Black Thunder. Alligator came up so close behind the white man that Black Thunder almost knocked the white man to the ground when he nudged him with his head. The surprised white man turned around to see a dead alligator riding a big black horse! The white man's face was full of fear and no sound came from his open mouth. Alligator wore the alligator skull on his head! He snapped its jaws at the scared white man who took off running now through the woods screaming.

Hawk Eyes and Moses had their backs to Alligator and had not seen what had happened. They turned their heads just in time to see the scared white man running out of sight. They also saw *an alligator horseman*! They hugged the tree tighter, afraid for their own lives! However, when they looked back again it was Alligator taking off the alligator skull from his own head. They now all began to laugh!

"Well, you really scared that paleface good! He won't be coming back into these woods!" exclaimed Hawk Eyes.

"Well, I see your hunt was successful!" said Alligator as he untied their wrists and looked at the grazing cow nearby.

"Alligator, boy are we glad to see you! You saved my life again!" exclaimed Moses.

"Well, maybe. But if you had not caught the alligator skull this morning fishing...maybe I would not have been able to save you," said Alligator smiling at the skull now in his hands. "Thank you, Moses."

When they had safely returned from their hunt to Cuscowilla there were many new Indians to meet. One new arrival was an Indian half-breed boy named Osceola.

Chapter VII - Golden Friends Found

The sun shone brightly in the clear blue sky and into the eyes of the Seminole men as they built chickees for the new bands of Indians. These new Indians that joined the Seminoles fled to Florida when they lost their land and homes to the white men in Georgia.

"I warned them not to cross or cut a stick of my wood. That land, I warned them, was mine!" declared Neamathla to Micanopy as the two chiefs sat together on the floor of Micanopy's chickee.

"You are a good talker, Neamathla. I want you to talk to the white men for all of us. Maybe you can help the Seminoles when we meet the white men for peace talks at Moultrie Creek," said Micanopy.

"Yes. I will help you defend your land," agreed Neamathla.

"Good, then it is settled. We will leave for Moultrie Creek before the sun rises again. Come, let me introduce you to my Seminole advisers," said Micanopy as he led Neamathla to another chickee.

"You are come," greeted the Seminole advisers as they shook Neamathla's arm.

"This is Abraham, my slave. But he is also my interpreter. He tells me the words of the white men. He speaks for me to them. And this is Jumper; he was once a Red Stick warrior. He is my sense bearer and he is also married to my sister. And this is Alligator, one of my best warriors.

"I hope my proud voice will bring peace and quiet the war drums, for my people and for yours," said Neamathla to Micanopy's advisers.

Like the waves in the ocean, Seminole bands followed Seminole bands to Moultrie Creek. Their spirit was as strong as a mighty oak in the woods as they arrived and greeted one another. Many had never crossed each other's path before. The white men called the Indians – squatters.

"Alligator, I have met so many Seminoles: Black Dirt, Squirrel Jumper, Deer Foot, Rain Cloud, Grey Moon, Dandelion....my weak mind will never be able to remember all their names!" exclaimed Hawk Eyes as he and Alligator gathered wood in the forest for their campfire.

"Have you met Osceola or Wildcat (Coacoochee)?" asked Alligator.

"No ...maybe...I'm not sure," laughed Hawk Eyes.

"I have asked them to join us for dinner by our campfire tonight," said Alligator as he rolled over a log on the ground.

"WATCH OUT, ALLIGATOR!" shouted Hawk Eyes who was a dozen steps away.

All at once a large rattlesnake that was coiled up under the log sprang forward and bit Alligator on his right ankle.

The snake's poisonous fangs cut right through his moccasin boot. Alligator fell to the ground and the snake coiled up to strike again! Just as he rattled his tail and raised his triangle-shaped head, an arrow pierced his neck and the snake fell to the ground dead. Alligator looked up to see Moses standing over him with his bow just before his eyes closed and his world became dark. Luckily, Moses had just wandered upon them while hunting for a squirrel for dinner.

"We must find the Medicine Man!" declared Hawk Eyes as he and Moses picked up Alligator and ran back with him to the Indian camp at Moultrie Creek.

"Go back and find that rattlesnake!" ordered the Medicine Man when he saw Alligator's wound. "He needs its fangs for courage!"

"Here it is," said a small voice in the dark. It was Gold, the little person. He held the long dead snake in his small hands. The rattle snake was longer than Gold was tall. Gold walked through the crowd of Indians that had gathered around Alligator and the Medicine Man. Everyone stared at Gold as he walked forward dragging the long snake behind him. Many of the Seminoles had never seen a little person from the forest before and many were afraid of him.

The Medicine Man spoke to Gold first. "I need you to bring me my medicine bundle. It is hidden deep in the forest. Have you seen it?" asked the Medicine Man.

"Yes, but I will need someone to help me carry it. The medicine bundle weighs much more than me," explained Gold.

"I will go!" shouted Hawk Eyes with tears in his worried hawk eyes. "Alligator is my fellowhood brother. I will not let him die!"

"GO! Go fast! Your brother does not have much time!" ordered the Medicine Man and then he began sucking the poison from Alligator's wound and then spitting it out on

69

L.L. Eadie

the dry ground. Next, he scratched Alligator's skin with the rattlesnake's fangs to give him courage.

Gold rode on Hawk Eyes' shoulder, just as he had ridden on Alligator's. Hawk Eyes ran through the forest as if he had grown the wings of a great hawk.

"Slow down and listen. The forest will tell us where to look," said Gold.

"You mean to tell me that you don't really know where the medicine bundle is?" asked Hawk Eyes who was now panting and out of breath.

"Be quiet and listen," ordered Gold.

Hawk Eyes looked around him in the dark and saw nothing stirring. But all at once he heard the forest talking. The owl in the tree, the crickets in the shrub and the frogs in the swamp all called out to them the location of the medicine bundle.

"Inside the log," whooed the owl.

"Inside the log," chirped the crickets.

"Inside the log," croaked the frogs.

"There! There's the hollow log!" exclaimed Hawk Eyes pointing to it in the dark.

"I see it!" said Gold as he rushed to the log. Gold crawled deep inside it and when he felt the antler of a deer, he knew he had found the medicine bundle.

Alligator finally opened his eyes two moons later. The magic in the medicine bundle had saved his life! He looked around the chickee and saw many new faces and some old ones too. There were his new friends—Wildcat and Osceola and his old friends, Hawk Eyes and Moses. *And...Gold?*

"Gold is that you?" asked Alligator as he sat up.

"Yes. I have come for my gold that you owed me.

"Yes, I remember my golden friend," smiled Alligator. "Did you protect me from harm again?"

"Yes. and so did Hawk Eyes and Moses. I guess you owe them gold now too!" laughed Gold. Everyone laughed including Alligator.

Historical Summary - The First Seminole War - "The White Patriots Verses the Red Patriots"

The first Seminole War was labeled the "Negro Slave War." The American settlers were angry at the Seminoles for recruiting more runaway slaves to Florida. One problem that helped conflicts arise between Inidans and whites were the poorly defined border between Florida and Georgia. This often caused confliects such as cattle rustling by the Indians.

The first major battle of the war was September 27, 1812. Colonel Daniel Newman from Georgia along with a volunteer force from Georgia of 117 men fought King Payne and seventy-five Seminole warriors. The battle lasted eighteen days. Firfty Indians were killed and eighty-year-old King Payne died from his injuries a few months later. Newnan returned to Georgia a hero and one of the largest territorial towns in north Florida was named after him – Newnansville. It no longer exists today. However, there is a shallow lake named after him – Newnan's Lake. It lies close to the spot where the battle took place just north of Payne's Prairie. A couple of months later another American force along with Tennessee volunteers that outnumbered the Seminoles in the area four-to-one destroyed the Indians' homes, crops, belongings, and took many head of their cattle and horses. During this devastating three-week campaign one American and twenty Seminoles perished. Again, the Americans returned to Georgia as heroes.

The Seminoles were considered now no longer a threat to Georgia. It was not safe in northeast Florida any longer for the Seminole Indians. Territorial law gave white men the right to punish, not kill, Indians for stealing or killing their livestock and for enticing slaves to runaway. White patriots took over the Seminoles' land and killed any Indians they found on it. However, the Seminoles developed a new kind of warfare we call today "guerilla." The Indians traveled only at night in small groups of four or five men. They often ambushed the white men at nightfall.

After King Payne's death his brother, Bowlegs, became chief for a few years. He moved the town, which was a custom when a chief died, from Payne's Town, which was located at today's Payne's Prairie south of Gainesville, Florida to "Bowlegs' Town" ten miles southwest of Payne's Town. Bowlegs spoke at King Payne's funeral – *"What is passed and cannot be prevented should not be grieved for. What a misfortune for me that I could not have died instead of you. What a trifling loss our people would have sustained in my death; how great in yours."* The next chief was Long Tom for a short time until his death. Micanopy succeeded his brother, Long Tom.

The sinkhole at Payne's Prairie was known by the Seminoles as the "Big Jug" or "Alachua" because waters were constantly flowing into it but never filling it. The Indians pronounced it "Ala-cue-ah." Today it is commonly pronounced "Uh-loch-chew-ah." The word *Alachua* today refers to a small north Florida town and also to the entire county surrounding Gainesville, Florida and Payne's Prairie, which is a state preserve today comprised of over 20,000 protected acres.

The Seminoles had a polytheistic religion. Some of their important gods were "Pohyah" the creator or great spirit, "Hesaketa" the breath of life, and "Tumese" the giver of life. When a Seminole died it was the custom to clad the man's body in a new buckskin shirt, a red handkerchief and a turban. All other clothing of the dead was bundled up and carried away. Only items of value to his next of kin were kept. All other evidence of his existence was disposed of. King Payne requested that his white horse be saved and given to his daughter. The Seminole coffin was made of palmetto logs and a blanket was wrapped around the deceased and placed inside along with broken possessions. The coffin was protected by two thatched lean-to roofs. Only the women were permitted to cry. Seminole Indians never buried their dead together in a cemetery. The Seminoles feared the ghosts that might be haunting the graveyard. They believed the ghosts might try to get your spirit.

Other new faces in Florida included Osceola, who moved to Florida when he was about the age of nine years old along with his mother, Polly, a Red Stick Creek Indian and his uncle, Peter McQueen. Osceola's father was an Englishman named William Powell. Osceola had his father's light eyes. Osceola's English name was Billy Powell. His family settled along the Peace River in Florida.

The Red Sticks or Upper Creek Indians had been defeated by General Andrew Jackson in the famous battle of Horseshoe Bend. Andrew Jackson earned the nickname "Old Hickory" because of his iron will and determination. However, the Indians called him "Sharp Knife" and when Jackson became president of the United States, they referred to him as the "Great White Father."

Many Red Sticks migrated into Florida. Another Red Stick Indian that moved there was Neamathla. He had settled near the border of Florida and Georgia and was attacked and forced into the Florida swamp lands. Neamathla was selected by the Seminoles to be their spokesman at the Moultrie Creek Treaty conference meeting. Moultrie Creek is located about five miles south of St. Augustine, Florida. Seventy Seminole chiefs and 475 Indians attended the seventeen-day Moultrie Creek conference. Thirty-two chiefs signed the Moultrie Creek Treaty.

Abraham was an important Seminole Maroon leader. He was also chief Micanopy's interpreter and one of his top advisors. Abraham was intelligent and considered to be a chief among the Maroons. His knowledge of the white man's ways and language made him extrememly important to Micanopy. Abraham was born a slave in Pensacola, Florida. He joined the Seminoles at the approximate age of twenty-six.

Part III - The Second Seminole War: "Promises! Promises!"

Chapter I - The Promised Land Called the Reservation

A bark house was built for the peace talks between the Seminoles and the white men of Florida at Moultrie Creek. Seventeen moons later, a peace pipe was smoked, and a treaty was signed.

"Neamathla, when will your band be ready to move to our new promised land, called the reservation?" asked Micanopy as the two chiefs prepared to leave Moultrie Creek.

"Didn't Abraham tell you? My band is moving west on other land in Florida. It is a much smaller reservation than yours," said Neamathla as he climbed onto his horse.

"No, he didn't. Why aren't you and your band going with us?" asked Micanopy, who was standing next to his own horse.

"We are not Seminoles. We don't belong on your reservation," explained Neamathla. "Besides, I am too old to move."

"You are always welcome to join us. Thank you for your wise words here at Moultrie Creek. We will meet again," said Micanopy.

Chief Micanopy stood and watched Neamathla and his band of Indians slowly ride away into the sunset. Their paths would never cross again.

"I am afraid the white man is like a lying rabbit. He could have tricked us! We might have made a bad trade," said the worried Alligator to Micanopy's other two advisers, Jumper and Abraham. The three Indians were riding their horses back home to Cuscowilla, later that same evening.

"Is there such a thing, as *bad* land?" asked Abraham.

"Yes," said Jumper. "Land that starves its people is a land with bars!"

"We won't starve. The white man promised us food, cows, and money," said Abraham.

"Yes. I hope you are right, Abraham," said Alligator.

When the Seminoles returned home, they packed their belongings and headed for their promised land, called the reservation. The elders dreamed of the good old days in paradise. A land where they could hunt and fish freely, grow crops, own herds of cattle, and celebrate the Green Corn Dance. The young Indians dreamed too of a land free of white men and the right to roam on their own land without fear. The Maroons also had a dream – a dream of a land that belonged to them and was where no slave catchers were allowed. Would this new promised land called, the reservation keep its promises? This was what was on the minds of all of the Seminoles as they traveled by foot, horseback and canoe to *their* promised land, called the *reservation*.

Four winters passed. The Seminoles' promised land called the reservation had kept few promises. However, the Seminoles had survived!

"Hello Alligator, I have good news! I am a father! exclaimed Hawk Eyes, as he held up his crying baby boy over his proud head to show him off.

"I am happy for you, Hawk Eyes! That is very good news! He looks just like you!" said Alligator who had just returned from the white man's fort, Fort King, with rations for the hungry Indians. "Hush Be Quiet has made you a good wife."

"Yes, and a good cook too...when we have food," said Hawk Eyes softly as he patted his son's back to calm his hungry cries. Hawk Eyes was ashamed that he could not provide enough food for his hungry family.

"Here, take this sack of flour and bags of seeds. Plant a garden for your new baby boy. Soon his cries will turn to laughter," said Alligator handing Hawk Eyes the two bags. Alligator noticed how thin his friend, Hawk Eyes, had become.

"I hope this garden will grow. It has not rained in a very long time," said Hawk Eyes as he made a sad face while looking up at the sun in the cloudless blue sky.

"Yes, that is so. The sun has always hated us. I wish my ears could hear the croaks of the tree frogs and alligators telling us that it's going to rain. I have an idea, why don't we perform a rain dance for the Great Spirit," declared Alligator smiling. He was hoping to raise the spirit of his fellowhood brother, Hawk Eyes.

"That is a wonderful idea! We should have thought of that before!" exclaimed Hawk Eyes as he swung his baby boy around in a circle. The baby boy stopped crying and giggled.

"Careful, you may drop him," teased Alligator smiling at his fellowhood brother's happy face.

"No! Never! He is too important to me! He gives me hope! *Hope* that our good life will return, like the flowers in the spring."

"Hope is good, Hawk Eyes. Hope helps make our hearts beat and our souls sing. I hope that our rain dance will stir the Great Spirit!" said Alligator as he smiled and held the small hand of *Hawk Eye's hope*, his baby boy.

Perhaps the Great Spirit did not hear the rain dance, for the skies stayed cloudless and blue. No thunder was heard. No lightening was seen. No showers were felt. The hateful sun continued to shine and shine and shine. It dried up the swamps and cracked the earth. The promised land called the reservation only brought broken promises of sickness, starvation, and death to the Seminoles. Sadly, the seeds of the garden never grew up and neither did Hawk Eyes' hope, *his baby boy* and many other Indian children. Alligator also suffered a loss also when his mother died.

Chapter II - The Return of White Lies

The white man's calendar read 1830 and Old Hickory, Andrew Jackson was now their Great White Father or president. The Seminoles knew Jackson as Sharp Knife. They knew too that just as the sun dries up the rain so will the white man take their land!

"I know our promised land, called the reservation has not been kind to us...but...it is all we have left of Florida, the village of many Indians. Can Sharp Knife force us off our land?' asked Moses.

"No! The Moultrie Creek Treaty we signed with the white men says this reservation is still ours for seven more years!" answered Alligator as the two of them sat by the bed of the sleeping Hawk Eyes in his chickee.

"What is it?" asked Hawk Eyes weakly as he opened his closed eyes. Hawk Eyes had been sick for many moons. He had rarely spoken, except in his deep hot sleep. Alligator and Moses were so worried that they had refused to leave his side.

"I am glad to see that you are awake my friend," answered the surprised, but happy Alligator.

"I will go and get the Medicine Man," exclaimed Moses excitedly as he rushed from the chickee across the small village to another chickee. The Medicine Man raced to Hawk Eyes' side with Moses. The Medicine Man had been very busy helping other sick Indians in their village. There was a sickness that had spread like poison ivy from chickee to chickee!

"Tell me about your dreams, Hawk Eyes," demanded the Medicine Man.

"I dreamed about hunting deer with my baby boy," answered Hawk Eyes with tears in his weak eyes, for he knew it was only a dream.

"I see...Hawk Eyes...you have visited the Happy Hunting Grounds...but the Great Spirit has sent you back to us! We are glad to speak with you again. Your friends, Alligator and Moses have waited for your return. I will now sing a special chant to keep your soul from leaving us again," said the Medicine Man and then he began to sing.

Hush Be Quiet came to see her sick husband as soon as everyone had left his side. Many of his friends had come to welcome his soul back home too.

"Hawk Eyes, it is good to see your hawk eyes again. I have brought you a dinner of palmetto cabbages and roots of plants. I am sorry...it is all I could find to cook," said Hush Be Quiet smiling.

Hush Be Quiet
(Taayai·yaktəl)

"Thank you. Don't be sorry, Hush Be Quiet. Did you hear? Good news! I was hunting with our little boy!"

"Yes). I wish we still had our baby boy here with us. I wish we still lived on our paradise. Our lands were once rich

81

with fields of corn, cows and animals to hunt. I wish we were still young and healthy dancing together at the Green Corn Dance. Do you remember the Steal a Partner dance, Hawk Eyes? That was when we first met."

Hawk Eyes just smiled and nodded his weak head. He did not speak. He knew Hush Be Quiet had more to say, just like a noisy gull at the shore, he could not stop her from talking. He listened and ate her meal of roots and cabbage to make him strong again.

"This promised land we call the reservation is full of too much suffering! It took our baby boy and it almost took you, Hawk Eyes! Maybe, Sharp Knife is right about this other new promised land called the *territory*. Maybe it is a paradise with plenty of good land and animals to hunt. What good is this reservation that we live on now? It gives us only broken hearts! My eyes are tired and red from tears that have flowed like a downhill stream. Maybe, Hawk Eyes, in this new land you can hunt deer with another son," pleaded Hush Be Quiet. She was now still and waited for his answer.

"Hush Be Quiet, my ears hear your sadness. My eyes see your sadness. My heart is broken for your sadness. But, listen and don't speak with your unhappy ears, eyes, and heart to my words. Maybe my small words will help you understand. This land belongs to our Seminole forefathers. The palefaces have returned with more white lies. They do not keep their word. Their tongues are forked. We signed a treaty with them at Moultrie Creek. But now they will not honor it! They bite the hand they shake, like a mad dog. This new land, called the territory is foreign to the Seminole. I have been told that white crystals called snow fall from the grey sky during the cold winters. It freezes the ground. We could perish here...or...there. *I choose here!*"

It was not long before the white man brought a new agreement to the Seminoles to sign; The Treaty of Payne's Landing. The white men believed the Seminoles would want to sign it. Hush Be Quiet was right, things had been bad for the Seminoles. The white mean believed the time was right. The Seminoles would now be ready to leave!

The same white man, James Gadsden, who had promised the Seminoles food, cows and money at Moultrie Creek now returned with new paleface promises from Sharp Knife.

"We can no longer feed you and protect you if you remain here. Life in the territory will be much better! There is plenty of good land. You will be free to roam on your own land again! You will be able to govern yourself and make your own laws," said the Indian agent, James Gadsden, at the meeting at Payne's Landing on the reservation.

"We do not have warm clothing for this cold territory," protested Jumper, Micanopy's speaker.

"I give you my word that each of you will be given a new blanket and shirt as soon as you arrive in the territory," promised the Indian agent, James Gadsden.

"The Moultrie Creek Treaty says we still have seven more years on this reservation in Florida, the village of many Indians!" declared Jumper.

"I'm not saying you have to leave tomorrow. You have three years before you have to leave to better land in the territory. We will buy your reservation land from you and any livestock you own. You can decide for yourself, if you want to travel by land or by boat," said the Indian agent James Gadsden.

"It seems to me that the white man will not rest until he has all our land!" exclaimed Jumper loudly with anger in his voice.

"If you stay, you will live by U.S. laws, not the laws of the Seminoles! I repeat...we will no longer protect you!" said James Gadsden, the Indian agent very loudly and angry too.

"The Treaty of Moultrie Creek said we could live in peace on that promised land called the reservation for twenty years! We were told that we would spend the rest of our natural lives there. You promised our lives would not end by white man's violence!"

"Don't be a fool! Your land here is no good! Your people are dying! We offer you paradise in the *Indian Territory*," said another Indian agent, Wiley Thompson. "Count your people, sell us your cows and horses, and board the boats peacefully!"

No one else spoke. Jumper turned to Micanopy and talked quietly and then he answered the white men, "Our chief, Micanopy, will *not* accept your offer ... *unless* ... Seminole Indians go and look with their own two eyes first at the Indian Territory. When they return, Micanopy will know then if you speak the truth or if you have returned with more white lies!

Chapter III - Indian Burn

The grey steamboat was anchored in the deep blue waters of Tampa Bay. The steamer's soon-to-be passengers included U.S. Major Phagan, seven Seminole leaders and a Maroon leader named Abraham. Long ago Abraham had run away from his white master and joined the Seminoles. His new master, Micanopy, the Seminole chief was his good friend. Micanopy trusted Abraham and had made him his interpreter. Micanopy depended on Abraham to listen and speak for him for the Seminoles to the white man.

"Abraham, how do you like being a slave?" asked James Gadsden, the Indian agent. He had seen Abraham standing alone by a wall at Fort Brooke in Tampa Bay before their steamboat left on its journey to the Indian Territory.

"It is not the same thing," answered Abraham. "I am not treated like a slave by my Seminole brothers.

"I see...then you must be a rich man, Abraham. Micanopy pays you well be be his interpreter, right?"

"No. He does not pay me."

"No? He doesn't? I'm surprised. You have a very important job!" said James Gadsden who was trying to trick Abraham into becoming a *renegade*.

"Yes, I do," agreed Abraham.

"And now he has asked you to go on this long trip and report back to him?"

"Yes," said Abraham who was now feeling confused.

"And he's not going to pay you anything?" asked James Gadsden.

"No," said Abraham now with a frown on his face.

85

L.L. Eadie

"Mmmm...I'll pay you!" said James Gadsden with a big smile. He then reached into his pocket and pulled out $200.00!

Abraham's eyes got big and his mouth opened wide at the sight of all that money. He had never seen so much money.

"Why would you pay *me?*" asked Abraham.

Abraham
(Souanakke Tustenukke)

"I want you to work for me, too," said James Gadsden looking around to make sure no one was listening.

"What would my job be?"

"This money is all yours, Abraham, if you make sure the Seminoles sign the treaty to move to the Indian Territory. Have you ever had this much money before?" asked James Gadsden waving the money in Abraham's face.

"No!" said Abraham shaking his head in disbelief.

"Do we have a deal, Abraham?"

"Ummm...I don't know."

"Yes or no?" demanded James Gadsden who was still waving the money in Abraham's face.

"Yes," said Abraham as he too looked around now to make sure they were all alone. But they were not! Someone was hiding and listening to their conversation. Abraham and James Gadsden never knew. This person was someone who could hide in places no one else could fit. Guess who?

The steamboat left that same day. Alligator, Hawk Eyes and Moses stood on the deck of the steamer and watched their ancient homeland disappear before their worried eyes. They had never been on such a big canoe!

"I'm scared, Alligator. Why did I let you two talk me into this?" asked Hawk Eyes.

"Don't be afraid. We will return home. I made sure of that!" said Alligator.

"Did *Gold* come?" asked Moses hopefully.

"Shhh...Yes. We don't want the others to know," whispered Alligator.

"Where is he? Where is he?" asked both Hawk Eyes and Moses looking around. They were both very happy to hear this news. Gold would protect them.

"I don't know. He is hiding," answered Alligator.

"What is it? Whose hiding?' asked Abraham as he joined them on the deck.

"*The fish*! I don't see any fish in this deep water. Do *you?*" asked the clever Alligator looking over the railing into the water pretending to look for fish.

"No," answered Moses as he also looked over the railing.

"No fish, not a one," agreed Hawk Eyes.

"Well, don't worry there will be plenty of fish in the Indian Territory," declared Abraham. He was already trying to impress the Seminoles about the territory.

"Alligator! Alligator! I have something very important to tell you," whispered Gold who was hiding inside Alligator's buckskin bundle.

"Shhh...not now...Shhh," whispered Alligator.

Days later as the seven Seminole Indians stood on deck, the steamboat paddled up a long muddy river to Fort Gibson. In the brown water they could see busy beavers building their dams.

"Did you see all those beavers?" asked Abraham trying again to impress the Indians. "Beaver fur is a good trade item."

"Yes," answered the Indians nodding their heads. Some were even smiling. Maybe the white man was right. This new reservation, called the Indian Territory might be their new paradise!

Chapter IV - Indian Guides

From the town of Little Rock the Seminole Indians followed Major Phagan on horseback to Fort Gibson. When they arrived at the fort, a pack of barking dogs greeted them. The dogs were followed by General Arbuckle and his soldiers. There were also a few foreign Indians there as well.

"My! My! My! What is it? What is all that noise?" asked Gold as he shook inside Alligator's buckskin bundle.

"It's only a pack of dogs," answered Alligator laughing at his little friend. He and the others rode their horses up to the pointed staked fence surrounding Fort Gibson.

"Well, they sound like a wolf pack! Be careful. Stay away from them. Dogs can make you sick! Alligator, I still need to tell you something very important!" said Gold.

"Shhh...not now...here comes the white man general," whispered Alligator.

"Eshtungo (Hello)," said General Arbuckle in the words of the Seminole as he walked up to greet the visiting Indians.

Alligator looked around at Fort Gibson as he and the others got down off their pack horses. There was a horse stable, a general store and several houses. The buildings were all whitewashed. Alligator wondered why. In the old-time Seminole village only the wise old men lived in white cabins.

Gold peeked out of Alligator's buckskin bundle that was now slung over his shoulder and looked around too. Gold began to shake with fear again.

"Gold, what is it? Why do you shake like the rattles of a snake?" asked Alligator quietly.

89

"Don't look! There's a graveyard over there!" whispered Gold ducking back inside the bundle.

"Did you see a ghost?" asked Alligator looking down at the ground now. He now was afraid too to look up for fear that he might see a ghost in the graveyard also.

"No," said Gold a little too loudly.

"Do you have two mouths?" asked one of the foreign Indians from Fort Gibson, who was now standing behind Alligator.

Alligator had not seen him walk up because he had been looking at the ground. Gold buried himself deep inside the buckskin bundle that rested on Alligator's back.

"No. I have only one mouth. Who are *you*?" asked the startled Alligator looking up now at the strange Indian.

"My name is Rabbit (Cho-fo-lock-sah). And that is my twin brother, Turtle (Yok-che)," said Rabbit pointing at his twin brother, who was now walking up very slowly to them. "We are going to be your Indian guides.

Alligator did not trust anyone named "Rabbit." A rabbit could never be trusted. He did not feel safe being around twins either. Twins were like thunder and lightning; don't ever make them mad! Alligator could feel Gold shake again now inside his bundle when he also heard the words – "rabbit" and "twins."

"Hello, Rabbit and Turtle. My name is Alligator. You two are not Seminoles Indians, are you?" asked Alligator.

"No. How could you tell?" asked Turtle as he slowly joined them.

"You wear the feather of the great eagle on your head. Seminoles do not," explained the clever Alligator.

"Good answer," whispered Gold to Alligator from inside the buckskin bundle resting still on Alligator's back.

Rabbit thought he heard the second mouth again. The second voice seemed to be coming from inside the bundle of this Seminole Indian who called himself Alligator. Rabbit wanted to sneak a peek inside that bundle! Thank goodness Gold was saved by the dinner bell!

"Welcome to Fort Gibson!" greeted General Arbuckle. "I know you are all hungry. Come inside and let's eat!"

The next day the twin Indian guides, Rabbit and Turtle led the Seminole party into the wilderness of the Indian Territory. In the woods they saw bears, wolves and panthers. In the prairies they saw wild chickens running about, wild horses, buffalo, and deer grazing.

"This Indian Territory sure looks promising, doesn't it?" asked Abraham still trying to impress the Seminole party.

The Seminoles had to admit the Indian Territory was very nice. It was springtime and there were wildflowers blooming everywhere. Suddenly...

"I see smoke," said Osceola, one of the seven Seminole leaders on the trip.

"Yes, it comes from the Creeks over that next hill," explained Turtle, who was slowly following the group.

"CREEKS?" shouted the seven startled Seminole leaders.

"I knew this place was too good to be true," whispered Gold peeking out of Alligator's bundle. "Alligator, I still have something to tell you!"

"Shhh...not now," said Alligator who noticed Rabbit staring at his backpack. Rabbit seemed to have the big ears of a rabbit also thought Alligator.

"The Creek Indians are the Seminoles' enemy," explained Abraham quickly to the twin Indian guides.

"You misunderstood my brother. Not the *Creek Indians*, but a creek...you know...a small stream of water. And this creek is full of fish!" exclaimed the lying Rabbit to the Indians.

"No. I did not misunderstand your brother! You are lying, Rabbit!" shouted Osceola madly.

"Never trust a rabbit," whispered Gold to Alligator.

"Are you calling me a liar?" asked Rabbit, who was now getting mad also.

"Yes," agreed Moses.

"Who are you, to call my brother a liar? You are a slave! Slaves will never be welcome in the Indian Territory!" shouted Turtle who was now mad too.

"He is a Seminole!" said Alligator defending his Maroon friend, Moses.

"Yes!" agreed the other Seminole leaders.

"Yes! Yes! You are both right! Moses and I are both Maroons. We are both slaves and Seminoles. Now, let's stop fighting. We should be using our eyes and not our mouths to look at this nice land. Our chief, Micanopy, is counting on us! Agree?" pleaded Abraham trying his best to calm everyone down.

"Don't trust Abraham," whispered Gold to Alligator.

"Yes," agreed most of the Seminoles, but not Alligator. He now wondered why the little person, Gold did not trust Abraham and why were the Creek Indians on there land-to-be in the territory. And what did Turtle mean when he said, "Slaves will never be welcome here!" There were just too many unanswered questions.

Chapter V - The Renegade

The whitewashed tombstones at Fort Gibson glowed like stars in the moonlight of the night. The dark shadows in the graveyard played tricks on the Seminoles' eyes. The visiting Seminoles were now ready to leave this place of forked tongues.

However, the white soldiers were not ready for the Seminoles to leave. There was still one more thing for them to see – the Treaty of Fort Gibson!

"Do not be restless, my Seminole brothers. Soon after sunrise we will all leave," said Abraham. He was the only Seminole who knew about the surprise treaty. Abraham wondered to himself as he lay down for the night with his Seminole brothers how he could convince them to sign the Fort Gibson Treaty. Abraham did not have Micanopy's permission and neither did the others.

When the wax of the candles had almost melted away, Alligator stirred awake. He could not find sleep, so he rose with his buckskin bundle and went outside to wait on sunrise. He was eager to leave this place and return to Florida, the village of many Indians.

"Gold, wake up," whispered Alligator into his bundle that now lay by his side on the ground.

"What is it?" asked Gold yawning. He had been asleep.

"The secret...what is it...tell me," said Alligator. "We are finally all alone."

"Oh, so *now* you want to know. I tried and tried to tell you before, but it was always, 'shhh, Gold, not now Gold, later Gold," teased his little friend.

"I am sorry, Gold. Please tell me," begged Alligator.

"Mmmm...let me see if I can remember...mmm," said Gold putting his small fist under his tiny chin pretending to be thinking. He stared up at the stars in the sky.

"Okay! Take these gold beads. They are all yours! You have kept us safe from harm. Now, tell me the secret," said Alligator smiling at his good luck charm while handing him the string of gold.

"Thank you, you didn't have to do that. I would have told you...maybe," laughed Gold putting on his new gold beads.

"Well?" smiled Alligator waiting on the secret.

"Okay, okay, what's the hurry? Don't rush me!" said Gold winking at Alligator. Suddenly Gold's silly mood changed, and he became very serious and stopped smiling and said, "The secret is this - there is a Seminole renegade among us here!"

"A renegade?"

"Yes."

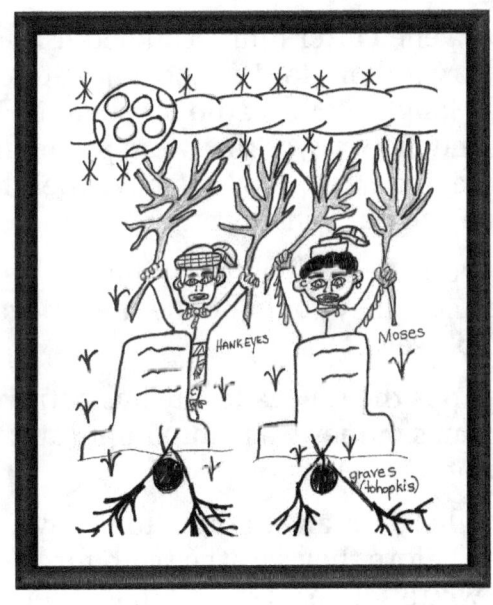

95

"Who? Tell me who would turn their backs on their Seminole brothers?" demanded Alligator whose own smile was gone now as well.

Suddenly...

"I knew it! My ears did not fail me! There are two mouths! One belongs to you, Alligator and the other to that little person you have been hiding in your bundle!" exclaimed Rabbit who stood up now from behind a tombstone in the graveyard where he had been hiding all along. Rabbit had secretly followed Alligator outside. However, he was not the only one who had followed Alligator!

"Well, your eyes must be failing you, Rabbit, because there is a ghost right behind you!" exclaimed Alligator pointing.

Rabbit turned around slowly and saw two tall dark shadows with very long arms and very, very long fingers coming close to him. He was so frightened that he took off just like a jack rabbit!

Alligator yelled after him, "You better find a Medicine Man in a hurry Rabbit, for the ghost has stolen your spirit!" He and Gold laughed and so did Moses and Hawk Eyes. It was Moses and Hawk Eyes that were pretending to be ghosts by swaying tree branches above their heads, making scary sounds and dark shadows.

"Thank you," said Alligator smiling at his two good friends. He knew they could not be the renegade. "Come and listen to Gold's secret."

"Abraham is the renegade! He has betrayed all of you! The white man's money was more important to him than his Seminole brothers!" exclaimed Gold.

This was hard for any of them to believe. However, it was not long before they saw the truth for themselves. At sunrise the white soldiers refused to let them leave the territory as they had promised to do. And Abraham did not help his Seminole brothers!

"You can not keep us here!" exclaimed the Seminole leader, Jumper to Major Phagan and General Arbuckle.

"We need you to sign this treaty before you leave," explained General Arbuckle.

"Treaty? What treaty?" asked another Seminole leader, Osceola.

"The Fort Gibson Treaty," answered Major Phagan.

"This treaty only says that we liked the land," explained Abraham to his Seminole brothers.

"But...we can not sign this," said Alligator shaking his head.

"The Indian Territory can be part ours! We won't have to share this good land *if* we sign. Don't you remember the black bears, wolves, panthers, chickens, horses, buffalo, and deer we saw? Don't you remember the sick and hungry families we left behind?" pleaded Abraham.

"We came to see this land *only!* When we return home we will tell our chief, Micanopy, what we saw. Then it will be decided by the tribal council if we come to live in the Indian Territory!" explained Jumper, Chief Micanopy's speaker.

"The only treaty I will sign is with this!" shouted Osceola as he stuck his knife into the treaty and stomped out of the room!

"Let's not get mad and fight. We are all just tired and homesick," said Abraham calmly.

"Yes, you are all very homesick," agreed General Arbuckle. "You do all want to go home...*don't' you?*"

"Yes," agreed the confused Seminoles.

"Well...then...you better sign this treaty or else..." warned General Arbuckle.

"Listen, my Seminole brothers, all this treaty says is that you like the land that you saw here *not* that you agree to move and live here," explained Abraham who knew he was tricking his brothers.

The Seminoles were afraid not to sign the Fort Gibson Treaty. They may never see their families again. How could they ever find their way back to Florida, the village of many Indians? They hoped Abraham was telling the truth and was not the renegade that Gold said he was.

Chapter VI - Shame on You, Abraham

A storm was brewing in the land of the Seminoles. Booming together in the distance were the drums of the Seminole warriors and the thunder of their gods. Their campfires lit their angry faces as the lightning lit the angry sky. Rain began to fall hard on the Seminole warriors, hiding the tears that fell from their unhappy eyes.

The white men had tricked the Seminoles again! Now the white men declared that the Treaty of Fort Gibson said that not only did the Seminoles *like* the Indian Territory *but* that they also wanted to move there!

"Chief Micanopy, we are sorry for signing our names to that treaty. We did try to tell them that we could not sign it," said Jumper.

"They would not let us come home if we didn't sign it!" explained Moses.

"Abraham said it was okay to sign the treaty. He told us the treaty said we just liked the land, not that we wanted to move there. Abraham is a renegade! It is entirely his fault!" exclaimed Wildcat.

"Yes!" agreed the other Seminoles.

"Alligator knows the truth about Abraham," said Hawk Eyes.

"Speak, Alligator. Tell me what you know," demanded Micanopy his chief.

"Gold told me that Abraham was paid to be the palefaces' friend. Abraham will regret his decision," explained Alligator sadly. Alligator knew how much his words would hurt his chief and he regretted having to speak them.

"Yes," agreed the Seminoles. "Shame on Abraham!"

99

"I see...that explains why Abraham has not returned. Alligator, I would like to talk to the little person you call by the name of Gold," said Micanopy, the Seminole chief.

"Yes, I will tell him when I see him next. He is hiding now from the thunder and the lightning," explained Alligator,

"Thank you, Alligator. I trusted Abraham. He was a good Seminole. I hear what you tell me, but my heart will not listen," said their upset chief, Micanopy.

"There is nothing left for us to do but fight for what is ours!" exclaimed the mad Osceola.

"Yes!" agreed the Seminoles.

"It saddens me to say these words aloud...but...Abraham has given me no other choice. I need twenty warriors to go and capture him and bring him back to me. If he resists...protect yourself! Shame on Abraham!" exclaimed Micanopy, Abraham's chief and good friend.

Chapter VII - Good-bye Abraham

In the morning a pretty rainbow had stretched across the clear blue sky. Last night's raindrops glistened on the leaves of the trees and every blade of grass. It was hard to believe that there was unrest in such a peaceful place.

"Don't point at the rainbow," warned Gold as he came out of the forest to find Alligator sitting on a log by the campfire eating corn soup (sofkee).

"Why?" asked the startled Alligator as he looked up to see his little friend walking towards him.

"Because if you do you will never be able to bend your finger again," laughed Gold.

"Really?'

"Yes, but if you don't believe me...go ahead and try it," said Gold smiling.

"No, I'll take your word for it, just as I took your word about Abraham. Chief Micanopy wants to talk to you."

"I know I already spoke to him last night after the rainstorm. Abraham has hurt your king, Micanopy, very deeply."

"Yes, twenty warriors left to find Abraham and bring him back...dead or alive!" explained Alligator.

"Yes, your king told me. He also said you will be leading the warriors on the warpath. I am very proud of you, my friend. You will make a good war chief!" declared Gold.

"Thank you," said Alligator.

It was not long before the twenty warriors returned to their chief's camp with Abraham.

"Is it true, Abraham? Are you a renegade?" asked Micanopy, when the two were alone in the king's chickee.

"Yes, my king. I am sorry that I have betrayed you and my Seminole brothers. Will you ever forgive me?"

"No! My warriors have told me that you are now an Indian guide for the soldiers of the Great White Father. Is this true, Abraham? Do you really lead the palefaces to our secret camps?" asked Micanopy.

"Yes. If I don't help them, my chief, my family will be sent back to their white masters. I will not let them be slaves again. Please, understand, Micanopy. I am still a Seminole and you are still my king. One day, I hope to return. But, for now, I will protect my family so they can be free," explained Abraham with tears in his dark eyes.

"Go! Do not come back! I have set you free. But if my warriors find you again...they will have an order from me to take your life!" cried the very upset Chief Micanopy. He felt like he had lost a son.

"I can only hope and dream of returning. If I have to wait forever, for a favorable sign from you, I will, my king!"

With those final words Abraham disappeared into the forest never to be seen by Micanopy or his clan again. If Abraham had hoped for the forgiveness medicine, that would make someone forget your sins against them, he never got it from the Medicine Man.

Chapter VIII - Warpath

As the time grew closer and closer for the Seminoles to leave Florida, the village of many Indians, tempers rose. Some Seminoles wanted to go to the Indian Territory, but most did not. Now the Seminoles argued with each other. Some even turned their backs on one another! These were confusing times for the Seminoles.

"We must stay together. Divided we are as weak as a broken arrow, but together we are as strong as the wind that comes before the storm," begged Chief Micanopy who sat on the west side of the council circle.

"Yes," agreed the Seminole leaders and warriors.

"Alligator has been chosen to be your war chief, a tustenuggee. He will be your teacher. Alligator Warrior (Halpatter Tustenuggee) will train you to crawl like a panther, close to the ground, to walk with no footsteps or footprints, and to camouflage your bodies like a green chameleon resting on a spring leaf."

All the eyes of the young warriors now fell on Alligator Warrior, their tustenuggee. Moses and Hawk Eyes were very proud of their friend. Although, Alligator Warrior was shorter than most of his warriors, he stood taller!

Alligator Warrior rose and placed a red two-foot-long war club in their village square to signal war! The war drums began to beat. The drums pounded all night. They would not stop until all the Seminole warriors had arrived.

Alligator was honored to have been chosen and named "Alligator Warrior." There were other great tustenuggees that had been selected before him. He knew that he must go and find a quiet place to think. There was much for his head to remember. He thought to himself, "What did my wise elders and uncle teach me that I must now teach the young ones?"

Alligator Warrior sat alone in the dark on a large rock in the woods. There were smaller rocks around him on the ground that shone in the moonlight. All at once these small shining stones began to tremble. Alligator Warrior rubbed his surprised eyes and looked once again. The small rocks now began to roll. They rolled down a narrow dirt path. Alligator got up and followed the glowing rocks. He was not afraid. These small stones could not hurt him. The path disappeared and the rocks stopped and so did Alligator Warrior. He could hear, but not see, an owl screeching up high in a very old tree. Alligator Warrior knew not to answer the owl's cries, for if one did, he may die!

Suddenly, a beautiful panther stood next to Alligator Warrior. He had not seen or heard the panther approaching.

"I've been waiting on you, Alligator Warrior," purred the panther.

"You have?" asked the surprised Alligator Warrior. He now felt fear tremble in his bones, yet he did not turn tail

and run.

"Yes. You do need to know how to swim like a fish, be brave as a bear, run like a deer, be tricky as a rabbit, or quiet as a snake in the grass, *and* as smart as the 'all-knowing' panther! *Don't you, Alligator Warrior?*"

"Yes!" exclaimed Alligator Warrior. The fear had now left his body and was replaced with excitement.

The panther said, "Well, I have been waiting to teach you. Are you ready?"

"Yes! Thank you! I am ready to learn 'all-knowing' panther!"

Alligator Warrior stayed with the beautiful panther all night! He had no time for sleep. There was too much to learn. The next morning Alligator Warrior returned to camp to teach his Seminole braves all that he had learned. Alligator Warrior now knew what to say and do!

"Don't be afraid...the powers above will take care of you!" said Alligator Warrior to the warriors as they all sat in a large chickee. The warriors were not afraid. That is why they were called braves.

Alligator Warrior continued, "We will prepare for war for three days. We will drink this war medicine given to me from the 'all-knowing' panther. I will teach you to be unseen and unheard. We will strike the white soldiers like lightning! And if they live to open their eyes, we will be gone from their sight!"

Chapter IX - War Party Plans

Three days had passed since Alligator Warrior began training the Seminole warriors for battle. He had taught the braves everything he had learned from the "all-knowing" panther. There was just one more day left before the war party. This last evening while the warriors slept in the chickee, Alligator Warrior laid awake planning their attack on their enemy, the white soldiers. However, the snores of the sleeping braves kept Alligator Warrior from coming up with a good plan. "Again, I must find a quiet place to think," thought Alligator Warrior. So, he got up to search for the right spot. He walked through the Seminole village but in every chickee there was someone snoring loudly. Alligator Warrior finally gave up and lay down by the campfire. He rested his head on one of the logs that stuck out of the warm fire. "Finally, quiet!" he said. However, it was not quiet for long.

"Hello," said Black Snake, the oldest Seminole Maroon in the Wahoo Swamp Village. No one knew for sure just how old Black Snake really was. He was at least one hundred years old!

"You are come," greeted Alligator Warrior as he jumped up quickly to shake arms with Black Snake. Alligator Warrior knew to show respect to his elders.

Black Snake reached for the wooden spoon in that day's stew pot that still hung over the fire. He slurped the soft corn soup called sofkee. Alligator Warrior thought it was a good thing that there wasn't any deer meat left...because Black Snake had very few teeth left for chewing in his old wrinkled mouth.

"Long, long ago, Alligator Warrior, I too was a tustenuggee. The day of our battle my braves and I painted our bodies the Seminole colors of war, red and black. We took off our turbans, neck scarves, and shirts. We wore very little.

"I don't understand, Black Snake. Your enemies must have seen you. How did you hide?" asked Alligator Warrior. He now sat up on the log across from Black Snake. Alligator Warrior was anxious to hear more. Black Snake may be able to help him with his war party plan.

"We wore the mud on the path and the moss from the trees. Our enemies walked right beside us and never even saw us!" explained Black Snake shaking his head and smiling proudly.

"Yes, that is good advice. Thank you. What was your battle plan, Black Snake?" asked the hopeful Alligator Warrior.

However, Black Snake only answered with a snore. The old man had fallen asleep after he had filled his hungry belly.

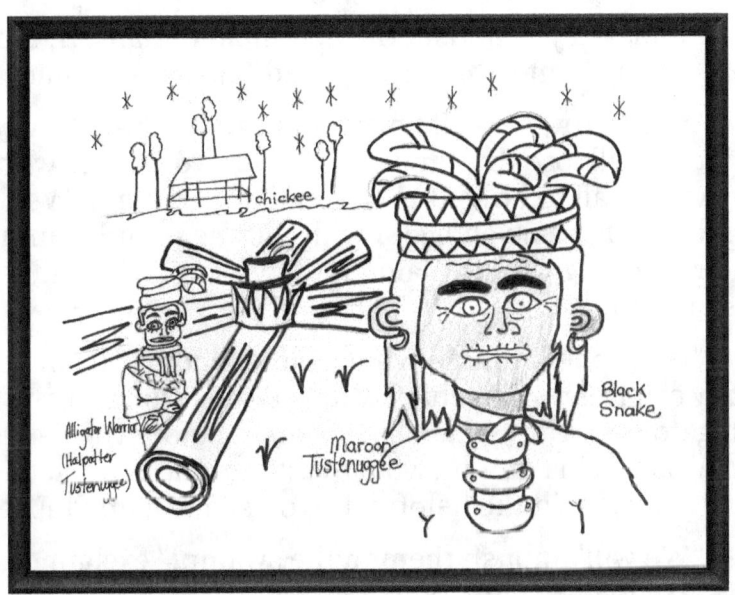

Alligator Warrior got up and covered Black Snake with a black bear hide. There was a chill in the air tonight. He left the snores of the campfire and walked out of the sleeping village. There wasn't much time left in the dark of night before daybreak. Alligator Warrior needed a war party plan. He had not gone far when he came to the bank of the Wahoo Swamp. All he could hear now were the croaking frogs. Suddenly, the dark swamp water began to boil, and a serpent appeared!

"It has been a long time since I last saw you, Alligator. Do you remember me? We met at the Big Jug. You were just a boy then," said the dragon snake as he swam up to the bank where Alligator Warrior stood.

"Friend!" exclaimed Alligator. He was not only happy to see Friend but also relieved that it wasn't a mean serpent!

"Where are your friends? Moses and Hawk Eyes? And the little person you called Gold?" asked the dragon snake, Friend, smiling wide and showing his two big fangs.

"Moses and Hawk Eyes live here in the village, but Gold lives in the woods somewhere. I don't know where though."

"I missed you and all the Seminole Indians. I, too, had to leave my home, the Big Jug, and find a new home."

"Tomorrow we will fight for our old homes. If we don't fight we will lose this land too. In three days, the white men say we are all to be sent to the Indian Territory. We must fight! We have no choice! I will lead the proud Seminoles as their tustenuggee!" explained Alligator Warrior sadly, but also proudly.

"I saw one hundred white soldiers not far from here. They call their white chief, Major Dade. Don't worry, Alligator Warrior, you will hear them before you see them. They have a big gun on wheels, and they are dressed in blue buckskins," said the helpful dragon snake named Friend.

"We will ambush them in the swamp!" exclaimed the very excited Alligator Warrior.

"No, that's what they think the Seminoles will do. Do what they don't expect. That will be an ambush!" suggested Friend.

"Yes! You are right, Friend! Thank you! I know of just the place where there are few pine trees and palmetto bushes. I now have a war party plan!"

Chapter X - The Dade Ambush

Alligator entered the Wahoo Swamp Seminole village just as the sun entered the grey sky. Cold rain began to fall. Chief Micanopy and Jumper were waiting for Alligator Warrior. Also waiting were his good friends, Hawk Eyes, Moses and Gold.

"This is a good plan, Alligator," said Chief Micanopy after Alligator had explained his war party plans to them all.

"Yes," agreed Jumper and then he added, "That clearing is close to our village. If we need to escape, we will not have far to go."

Meanwhile on the sandy road not too far from the hidden Seminole camp were the white soldiers that Friend had told Alligator about the night before. They all wore big coats and carried guns called muskets. The cold winter wind and rain blew in their pale tired faces. The soldiers had been marching for five days from Fort Brooke. They were heading to Fort King.

In the lead was a Maroon Indian guide named Pacheco. He was showing the white soldiers the way through the spooky swampy lands of the Great Black River (Withlacoochee River). Behind Pacheco on horseback were Major Dade and one of his captains riding by his side.

The time had finally come for Alligator Warrior to lead his braves into battle. He had taught them everything he had learned from the "all-knowing" panther. He had showed them how to paint their bodies and hide just the way Black Snake had told him. He had shared his war party plan that the dragon snake, Friend, had helped him with. They were now all prepared to fight!

"Moses, I may need your help. Stay close behind my war party with your Maroon tribe...just in case," explained Alligator Warrior.

"Yes. Don't worry, my friend. I will always be there for you, just the way you are always there for me!" exclaimed Moses.

"Thank you, Moses," said Alligator Warrior. He next hugged his fellowhood brother, Hawk Eyes and said, "I will need your hawk eyes too!"

"Yes, I am always here for you too," said Hawk Eyes as he hugged Alligator Warrior.

Everyone was ready, but scared.

"What about me? Have you forgotten about your good luck charm?" asked Gold waving his short arms up and down.

"No, I would never forget you! Thank you, Gold, for coming too. I always feel safe when you are around and know that gold beads are around your neck too," laughed Alligator Warrior.

The Seminole warriors left the village behind them very early that morning. The younger boys stayed behind to protect the women, children and elders of their hidden camp in the Wahoo Swamp.

The warriors followed Alligator Warrior, their tustenuggee. They walked in his footsteps behind him in a single file line. The last brave hid their footprints. As the Seminoles walked silently through the woods they tried not to leave any trace. They jumped from log to log or walked backwards cleaning footprints from their path, just like the "all-knowing" panther had taught Alligator Warrior. The braves left no signs of their presence!

"This is the place! Hide yourselves well using what the good earth has placed here. And remember to wait for the signal – Jumper's whoop! King Micanopy will take the first shot," explained Alligator Warrior.

"Alligator Warrior do you hear that?" whispered Gold as they both hid in a tall pine tree. They wore the pine needles, moss, and branches of the tree for cover just as Black Snake had taught Alligator Warrior.

"Yes. It must be the wagon carrying their biggest gun called the cannon," answered Alligator Warrior quietly.

It was nine o'clock in the morning when Hawk Eyes spotted the white soldiers coming down the sandy road. "They're coming! They're coming!" he whispered.

Friend was right, it was an ambush!

Chapter XI - Battle of the Great Black River (Withlacoochee)

A victory celebration was held at the Seminole Indian village in the Wahoo Swamp. Not only did the warriors celebrate the Dade Ambush, but also Osceola's surprise attack on Fort King.

Alligator Warrior sat quietly and watched the young braves perform the war dance in the smoke of the fire. They were all very, very happy. However, Alligator Warrior did not feel like celebrating.

The next morning after a restless sleep Alligator Warrior headed for the great black river (Withlacoochee River) for a swim. Even though the winter air was cold, the water would feel warm. He dove in and immediately felt better. He swam with the fish and snapping turtles. He watched a big blue heron fly above his head and spoke to it, "You, bird, were the second animal behind the panther to take your place on earth, by our Creator, the grandfather of all things." He then looked around at all the river animals and added, "You are all lucky to be so free!"

"They are not really free. Do you think they don't have an enemy? Every breathing thing has an enemy, Alligator Warrior!" said the one-eyed alligator who was sunbathing close by on the riverbank.

"Hello, one-eyed alligator. I did not see you over there," said the surprised Alligator Warrior, who was now standing in chest-deep water. He knew the one-eyed alligator could have easily swum into the dark water and attacked him! *And still could!* He was relieved to see Gold suddenly appear from a hole in a gnarled old cypress tree on the opposite bank.

"Well, lookee there, if it isn't the one-eyed alligator," said Gold smiling with only his small head sticking out of the hole in the tree.

"So, it's Gold, Alligator Warrior's lucky charm. Don't worry I'm not hungry for revenge. But you better believe the white soldiers are!" exclaimed the one-eyed alligator looking up at Gold.

"We're not scared of those soldiers! Didn't you hear? Alligator Warrior ambushed and defeated one hundred soldiers! And he'll do it again!" bragged Gold as he now climbed out to sit upon a big limb that hung over the river.

"Yes, I heard. So, Alligator Warrior, you're a hero now. How does it feel?" asked the one-eyed alligator.

"It's hard being a hero. I don't feel like one. It's hard being a Seminole tustenuggee. I'm only a man. I didn't know war would be like this. I don't know if I can do it again," admitted the worried Alligator Warrior.

"Are you looking for answers, Alligator Warrior?" asked the one-eyed alligator.

"No. I just can't stop thinking about the bad side of war. These sad thoughts kept me up with the owls all night," explained Alligator Warrior as he walked out of the warm water and onto the riverbank across from the one-eyed alligator and sat down.

"Well, things are not going to get any better. The storm has only just begun to brew. For every white soldier that dies, four will replace him!" said the one-eyed alligator.

"Don't listen to him! You are the best warrior! The Seminoles will win this war!" exclaimed Gold excitedly.

Alligator Warrior looked up at Gold and smiled. He knew Gold was trying to make him feel better and give him encouragement.

"Alligator Warrior let the fresh waters clean your mind and body. Then your spirit will be refreshed," advised the one-eyed alligator.

With these wise words, Alligator Warrior again dove into the great black river (Withlacoochee River). He was no longer worried about the one-eyed alligator. However, Gold remained sitting up high on the tree limb watching the one-eyed alligator...*just in case!*

Three days later the one-eyed alligator's insight did come true. The white soldiers, almost eight hundred strong, marched into the Wahoo Swamp looking for the Seminoles, led by General Clinch! The one-eyed alligator was also right about the river's waters; they did bring Alligator Warrior's spirit back to life! He now had a new war path plan based on the wise words of Friend, the friendly dragon snake, *"Do what the soldiers don't expect!"*

"Pacheco, I need your help. You are an Indian guide. The white soldiers trust you. Now, the Seminoles want to trust you too," said Alligator Warrior when he was back in the village.

"Yes, you can trust me. You have all been so kind to me. Tell me, what I can do to help the Seminoles," said Pacheco, their captive from the Dade Ambush.

115

"I want you to go to the white soldiers and tell them you have escaped. Tell their white chief General Clinch you know where we are in the Wahoo Swamp and you will gladly guide them to us!" explained Alligator Warrior.

"You want me to lead them to *your hidden village?*" asked the surprised Pacheco.

"No, but I want the white soldiers to think that you are. I have planned another ambush right where you will lead them across the Great Black River (Withlacoochee River)," answered Alligator Warrior.

"I know just the right place. The water is shallow there and easy to cross," suggested Pacheco.

"No," said Alligator Warrior as he shook his head. "I want *you* to lead them downstream to where the water is *deep*. There will be a canoe there for them to cross the river in. Together they are as strong as a back bear. The only way to weaken them is to divide them. We will wait in the trees like panthers and stalk our prey and then pounce on them!"

"Yes! That will be an ambush!!" exclaimed Pacheco, the Indian guide.

Chapter XII - Ft. Dade to Ft. Brooke

Black smoke filled the sky over the Wahoo Swamp. The Seminole villages were being set on fire by a new white chief named General Jesup. The one-eyed alligator's prediction was coming true. There were not enough sticks on the ground to count how many white soldiers now were in Florida, the village of many Indians.

Seminoles ran like the deer, but many could only move like a turtle. The white chief General Jesup easily captured the slow-moving Seminoles: the old, the sick, the very young, and their mothers. His soldiers also took the Seminole's ponies.

Sadly, the time had come for Micanopy to speak the words no Seminole ever believed they would hear from his wise mouth. However, Micanopy could see in his Seminole brothers' glazed eyes how low their morale had become.

"Many moons ago, I was a boy, and so were you. We ran and chased the rabbits. We hunted the black bear and we fished the sweet clear waters. Today those waters are red with Seminole blood. Our land has become poisoned by the palefaces who refuse to leave us alone. I have spoken to the Great Spirit and it is time for us to leave."

"Yes," agreed the warriors.

"Jumper, Cloud, and Alligator Warrior; I call upon you three to help your Seminole brothers and sisters. We can no longer hide in the woods, being chased like dogs, both day and night. Meet with this new white chief who calls himself Jesup and make peace," said the sad Seminole Indian chief, Micanopy.

"Yes," agreed Jumper, Cloud and Alligator Warrior.

The Seminoles found the white chief at a new fort named Fort Dade. Alligator Warrior recognized the spot as where he and his braves had ambushed Major Dade, fourteen months earlier.

"We have come in peace to make peace," said Jumper.

"Agreed!" exclaimed General Jesup.

"Do not pursue the Seminoles or the Maroons. We are one of the same," said Cloud.

"Agreed!" exclaimed General Jesup again.

"We are all ready to begin our lives on our own land in the Indian Territory," said Alligator Warrior.

"Agreed!" exclaimed General Jesup for the third time.

The Seminoles and the Maroons began to pack what little belongings they had left and move to Fort Brooke. Once there, they set up two camps near a river and waited for the white man's big canoes to carry them to the Indian Territory.

Many moons went by as the Seminoles waited with heavy hearts.

"Hawk Eyes, I fear for our people. Many are sick with the white man's disease called measles. They grow weaker and weaker," said Alligator Warrior as he and Hawk Eyes sat on the bank of a pond so large you could not see to the other side.

"Yes, I know. I have more bad news to share with you, Alligator Warrior. The white man has tricked us like a rabbit! He plans to settle the Seminoles on the Creeks' land in the Indian Territory! The Creeks are our enemies! They have helped the white man, to hurt us, too many times!" exclaimed the very upset Hawk Eyes.

Suddenly Moses appeared running along the bank and exclaimed, "Alligator Warrior, the slave hunters are here! They have taken the Maroon mother, Yellow Jacket and her children, Rain Drop, Laughing Moon and Honey Bee! They claim the Maroons are *all* runaways! I'm scared!"

"Me too," admitted Alligator Warrior. "I will go and speak to Micanopy about all the white lies from the forked tongue of their white chief they call General Jesup.

Alligator Warrior walked away from the great pond and his worried friends. He feared for their safety and of his people. As Alligator Warrior walked down the path he thought he felt someone following him. He stopped and listened.

"Hello, Alligator Warrior!" said Gold.

"Hello Gold," said Alligator Warrior sadly. This was not the way he usually greeted his lucky charm.

"I know why you are so unhappy. I also know that you are on your way to speak to Micanopy. You want to ask him if the Seminoles can leave this place of white lies. Save your breath, Alligator Warrior. Your chief is too old, and tired. He is ready to leave Florida, the village of many Indians. He will not change his mind!"

"What about you, Gold? Are you going to the Indian Territory?"

"No. You forget, Alligator Warrior, I have family and friends here. Besides, we will be safe from the white man, because he does not believe we exist!" explained Gold.

Meanwhile, one hundred miles away there were two hundred Seminoles that refused to come to Fort Brooke. They also had heard all the bad news!

"How can we just sit here and let our Seminole brothers and sisters leave for the territory?" asked Osceola.

"If the white man disease does not take their spirits, the Creeks certainly will!" exclaimed Wildcat (Coacoochee).

"Yes! We must sneak into their camps and steal them into the night as quickly as an owl takes its prey!" exclaimed Sam Jones (Abiaka) their Medicine Man.

Just as the full moon hid itself behind a dark cloud the Seminoles led by Osceola snuck into the camps and freed their Seminole brothers and sisters!

Gold was right. Their chief, Micanopy, refused to leave. However, Alligator Warrior and the others refused to leave him behind! They raised him to his horse, as if he were a feather, and rode him away like a north wind.

When the big red sun rose the next morning General Jesup was surprised to find the Seminole camps deserted. He cried out with anger the most-deadly word, *"Extermination!"*

Chapter XIII - White Flags

The white chief's words were heard by many white men. Volunteers came to help General Jesup rid Florida, the village of many Indians, of the Seminoles!

The Seminoles stayed on the run like scared rabbits. At every turn there were more and more white men. It became more and more difficult for them to find food to fulfill their hunger pains. Seminole mothers hid their babies only to return to feed them like a mother bird. Sadly, sometimes when the mothers returned their babies were gone! Black bears, wildcats or panthers had stolen them! Many other Seminole children died of hunger and disease.

"Listen to me! I know we are a proud people. But soon there will be no children and we will be a *dead people*! We must swallow our pride for our children...they are our future existence!" exclaimed Micanopy.

"Yes," agreed the Seminole warriors.

"We will go to Fort King and talk to the white chief Jesup and ask him for a reservation in the everglades, the great grass waters (pay-hai-o-kee)," said Alligator Warrior.

And so a group of Seminoles went to Fort King with Alligator Warrior and made the reservation request.

"I will send your request to the U. S. Secretary of War," said General Jesup. "But in the meantime, whenever you want to come and talk to me use a white flag. That way I know you have come in peace and my troops will not fire at you. Return when you are ready to talk about your passage to the Indian Territory!"

"We will never be ready to go to the territory!" exclaimed Sam Jones, the Medicine Man.

And with those final words the Seminoles left. Time

carried on and as the wind changes direction from the south to the north, so did a Seminole leader, King Philip's Maroon slave, John Philip.

"Who did you say you are?" asked General Hernandez at St. Augustine, where John Philip had wandered north too.

"I am John Philip, the Seminole Maroon of King Philip. King Philip is married to Micanopy's sister and King Philip's son, Wildcat will be the next Seminole chief!" said John Philip proudly.

"Where *is* King Philip? You better tell me the truth! I will hang you if you don't! Those are my orders from General Jesup," exclaimed General Hernandez.

John Philip had no choice; he too had to become an Indian guide just like old Abraham had done many moons earlier. He led the white soldiers to King Philip's camp. King Philip was put in jail at Fort Marion in St. Augustine. Wildcat, King Philip's son and Blue Snake, another brave Seminole went to General Jesup to ask him, to spare King Philip. They waved the white flag as they were told. However, General Jesup had them arrested too!

"You told us to bring a white flag if we wanted to speak words of peace," complained Wildcat.

"I have your father in chains and now, you too, are my prisoner! But I am going to free you, Wildcat. Go and find Osceola, and lead him to St. Augustine. We will then discuss the reservation. I promise the soldiers will not fire at you if you come in peace - use a white flag!" exclaimed General Jesup.

Wildcat returned with Osceola and his followers under a white flag.

However, when they reached St. Augustine, General Hernandez's soldiers surrounded them. The Seminoles' guns were taken and so were they, to the old Spanish fort, where King Philip still sat in chains!

The news spread quickly: Wildcat, Osceola, Hawk Eyes, and Moses had been captured! The white man's white flag was just another white lie!

Many moons later...

"Alligator Warrior, Hawk Eyes and I have escaped!" exclaimed Moses as he and Hawk Eyes ran into the hidden camp of the Seminoles.

"My eyes are pleased to see my two friends! We should not have trusted this new white chief Jesup! The white men will never be our friends! My heart is sad for Wildcat, King Philip and Osceola," said Alligator Warrior.

The unhappy weeks passed as slowly as the land turtle crawls across the hot sands. But finally good news arrived!

"Alligator Warrior!" exclaimed Hawk Eyes. *"Look!"*

"What is it?" asked Alligator Warrior.

"Here comes Wildcat!"

Chapter XIV - Battle of Big Water (Okeechobee)

The Big Water (Okeechobee) Lake looked like an ocean to Alligator Warrior as he stood on a lovely hammock of trees surrounded by a marsh. His good luck charm, Gold, sat up high on a limb in one of the many tall cypress trees of the hammock. There was plenty of Spanish moss hanging from the trees for cover. There were also cabbage palms growing there. Tall saw grass grew in the swampy waters near by. Alligator Warrior looked very hard and long at his surroundings.

"So, have you decided on a new war party plan?" asked Gold.

"No, I am still in deep thought."

"Well, what's wrong with this place? It looks like a pretty good place," said Gold as he swung his small feet back and forth from up high in the tree.

"Yes, you are right, Gold. 'Old Rough and Ready' (Zachary Taylor) and his soldiers would not be able to ride their horses onto that swampy land over there," agreed Alligator Warrior. "But it would be hard to see them coming in that tall saw grass beyond the hammock."

"Well, duh! Why don't you cut the grass then?" exclaimed Gold.

"Yes!" agreed Alligator Warrior nodding his head and smiling.

"And from up here, you can see even see better!"

"I will let Hawk Eyes and my best sharp shooters hide in these tall cypress trees. They can use the Spanish moss to camouflage themselves!" exclaimed Alligator Warrior excitedly.

"Now you need a plan to get Old Rough and Ready and his soldiers to come to this very spot so you can defeat him!"

said Gold.

Alligator Warrior thought and thought. Finally, he said, "Pacheco, the Indian guide, will help us, just like he did before!"

Pacheco gladly accepted. The plan was for Pacheco to pretend to be herding the Seminoles' few horses and cows. The soldiers would find him by looking for the source of the smoke – his campfire, where Pacheco would be sitting all alone. The white soldiers would of course capture Pacheco and force him to tell them where the Seminoles were.

Meanwhile, the Seminoles cleared the saw grass, leaving nothing but muddy water.

"We will now hide ourselves, like a chameleon on a leaf, and wait patiently, as a spider waits for its prey in its web, for Pacheco to lead the white soldiers to us!" exclaimed Alligator Warrior proudly.

Alligator Warrior and his warriors hid in the hammock. To his left was Wildcat, and his braves, and to his right was Sam Jones, the Medicine Man, and his followers.

Pacheco was captured, just as planned, and taken to their white chief called Old Rough and Ready, also known as Zachary Taylor.

"What is your name savage?" asked Old Rough and Ready.

"I am Pacheco, the Indian guide."

"Good, then you can lead us to the redskins!"

"Yes, I know right where they are! They are only one mile from here, in a very dry place. But there are about 1,000, no, maybe 2,000 Seminoles there!" lied Pacheco as he had been told to by Alligator Warrior.

"Good! That must be all of them! We will capture them all and this long war will finally be over! And I will be a hero!" exclaimed Zachary Taylor, known as Old Rough and Ready.

Hawk Eyes called out like a hawk from up high in his tree to signal the Seminoles that the white soldiers were approaching. Not only were they easy to spot in their blue coats, just like the feathers of a blue jay, but also just as noisy as one!

The Seminoles could hear the soldiers' dogs barking as they tried but failed to cross the muddy water. The Seminoles fought bravely from the ground of the hammock to the tallest trees. The fighting lasted over two hours!

"Alligator Warrior, the medicine man, Sam Jones and his warriors have left you and Wildcat!" said the alarmed Gold as he hid under a cabbage palm as the battle carried on.

"Yes. We too will gather our wounded and dying, and so will the white man. But *we* will not surrender!" exclaimed Alligator Warrior as the Seminoles retreated deep into the hammock to fight another day.

Chapter XV - The Red Knight

There were no more bright happy mornings or pleasant gentle breezes for the Seminoles. Only broken tired hearts remained. Sadder words came to them each day. One day the message said that the Great Spirit had taken the great Seminole warrior, Osceola, into the Hereafter. The next day, more sad words - Micanopy's request for the reservation in the Great Grass Waters of the Everglades was rejected. Then, Jesup, their white chief, captured over 500 Seminoles and Maroons that were waiting for the reservation news close by.

A new Indian face emerged from the soft hidden trails of the Seminoles. He called himself a Cherokee. He explained to the Seminoles that the Cherokees too, had once lived in their own paradise in the mountains, and they too had been forced by the white man off their land to the Indian Territory.

"The territory has good land. You can be free there!" said the Cherokee Indian to the Seminole's chief, Micanopy and his followers.

"The white man has a forked tongue. He said the Seminoles did not have to live with our enemy, the Creeks. But he lied!" exclaimed Alligator Warrior.

"Come with me and tell the white chief that you will all leave Florida, the village of many Indians, if you can have your own promised land," said the Cherokee.

Micanopy listened with his tired old heart to the Cherokee's words. He believed his words were not lies. The Cherokee Indian led Micanopy and Alligator Warrior, and their band to the white chief General Jesup, under a white flag. Again, Jesup proved his word was that of a mad dog. He imprisoned them all!

"Go if your spirit says you must," said the sad Micanopy

127

to Alligator Warrior.

"I thank you, Micanopy, for not only being a good chief but also my friend. You have been like a father to me. We will meet again!" said Alligator Warrior before he escaped leaving behind his old chief.

Alligator Warrior's heart was heavy as he walked under the moon and stars in search of Wildcat, and his clan, in the Big Cypress Swamp.

"You are come, Alligator Warrior," greeted Wildcat happily when Alligator Warrior had found his hidden camp.

"Thank you, Wildcat. My, my...what fancy clothes you are wearing!" complimented Alligator Warrior with a smile. It felt good to smile again.

"Yes! Thank you! I took them from a white man's wagon," said Wildcat smiling proudly at his new costume. He looked like *Romeo* from the white man's play *Romeo and Juliet*.

The Seminoles led by Alligator Warrior, Wildcat, and Sam Jones, the Medicine Man, continued to fight for

Florida, the village of many Indians, for the next three years. Sadly, the next Seminole to wear the white man's chains was Wildcat, their next chief!

"I am about to leave Florida forever, and have done nothing to disgrace it. It was my home; I loved it, and to leave it is like burying my wife and child!" said the sad Wildcat to his clan, including Alligator Warrior, who would follow him to the Indian Territory.

Chapter XVI - Stone Faced Savages

The white man's big canoe rocked back and forth as the blue waters splashed hard against its side. The grey sky cried for the sad Seminoles as they left Florida, the village of many Indians. The rain's teardrops streamed down the stone faces of the Seminoles as they sat on the wooden deck. It is hard to say if their bodies shivered from the cold or from fear. The white soldiers now seemed to feel the Seminoles' despair and handed them each a blanket. The Seminoles spoke no words. The only sounds that could be heard were the blowing wind, crashing waves, and the cries of the Seminole mothers for their lost children!

The air smelled different in the Indian Territory. This was no paradise for the Seminole Indians. No fertile land, full of game, awaited them here. In fact, there was no land for them at all!

"How can we share this land with our enemy, the Creeks?" asked Wildcat, madly.

"Their laws are *not* our laws!" exclaimed Gopher John a Seminole Maroon, and a close friend of Wildcat's. "I am worried the Creeks will make me and my brothers and sisters slaves again."

"The Maroon are Seminoles too!" exclaimed Moses, who was also concerned. "I am moving my clan to the Cherokee land. They will be safer there."

"The Seminoles that have come before us have forgotten Wildcat!" exclaimed Alligator Warrior.

"You should be the Seminole chief!" declared Hawk Eyes to Wildcat.

"Yes!" agreed Wildcat's band. However, another Seminole was now chief in the Indian Territory. His name was John Jumper.

"They have all turned a blind eye, and deaf ear to me. They say we are no longer in Florida, the village of many Indians. I have tried and I know you have too, to make this foreign land our home, a place once like King Payne's. The white man gave us his word. His word breaks like glass. It is time for us to leave. Who will follow my trail?" asked Wildcat.

Chapter XVII - South of the Border

And so, when the owl awoke, Wildcat along with Alligator Warrior, Gopher John, and their clans left the Indian Territory, as quietly as a baby deer hides in the woods.

"Your name, Wildcat, should be *Moses* too. You, Wildcat, will lead your people, just like Moses did in the Good Book in search of a new land to call their home!" exclaimed Moses.

"Yes," agreed Alligator Warrior. "I remember, Moses, when I was just a boy, you telling me that story the first time we met."

"We were both boys. Thank you for everything you have done for me Alligator Warrior. You have been a good friend. Now, together we will find a place we can both call home," said Moses, as the fleeing Seminoles walked far away from the Indian Territory, and Florida, the village of many Indians.

"Look up ahead!" exclaimed Hawk Eyes. "There are people."

"I hope they are not slave hunters!" exclaimed Gopher John.

"No. They are Indians," said Hawk Eyes.

"I could always depend on your hawk eyes!" said Alligator Warrior smiling.

"Yes, and I could always depend on you too. You were there the night I met my wife, Hush Be Quiet at the Green Corn Dance, when we received our names. And, how can I forget how you helped my sad broken heart when the Great Spirit came for my baby boy?"

"Yes. We have had a fellowhood. We are friends for life. We have always protected each other from harm," said

Alligator Warrior.

The strange Indians now came closer and greeted the Seminoles. The two tribes had never crossed paths before. These Indians called themselves the Kickapoos. They made friends with the Seminoles and decided to follow Wildcat's trail to Mexico too. The Seminoles and the Kickapoos traveled a long, long time until they finally reached a river.

"We will build rafts and cross here," declared their chief, Wildcat.

"Yes," agreed the Indians as they cut down trees to make rafts that would swim like fish across the deep water.

The skies turned black and rain fell hard from the sky south of the border. The Seminoles along with the Kickapoos used long sticks to push the rafts across the river to their new home, Mexico. First, mothers and children crossed the river, and then their brave fathers and big brothers. Once everyone was safely across their chief, Wildcat spoke to them.

"We have traveled a long way brothers and sisters. No longer will we have to listen to the white man's forked tongue! No longer will the slave hunters steal away our mothers, fathers, and children! No longer will our babies go hungry and starve! No longer will the white chiefs take our horses and cows. We have fought hard and lost much. But now we can proudly say that we are free and that we are home!"

The End

Historical Summary - The Second Seminole War "Promises, Promises"

The Treaty of Moultrie Creek was signed by thirty-two Seminoles and three government representatives, one being William P. Duval who was the territorial governor of Florida. The treaty was ratified by the U.S. government on December 23, 1823. The Moultrie Creek Treaty was a poor bargain for the Seminoles. The Seminoles only received three quarter of a cent per acre. They gave up twenty-four million acres of the best land in Florida for 4,032,490 acres of the worst land. The soil was difficult to farm and there was an absence of animals and plants that the Seminoles were accustomed to. The treaty allowed white settlers to only pass throught the Seminole reservation for lawful purposes. The white settlers were not allowed to hunt on the Indian's reservation. White settlers and slave catchers ignored the treaty agreement and entered the Seminole land. Violence often erupted. The Moultrie Creek Treaty granted the Seminoles this land for a reservation for twenty years. This reservation was located fifteen miles south of Ocala and extended to Lake Okeechobee. The reservation was also fifteen miles inland from the gulf coast and twenty miles inland from the Atlantic Ocean.

The Seminoles moved to the Wahoo Swamp, which is located eighty miles to the north-northeast of Tampa and around the Withlacoochee River, and also Bushnell in Sumter County Florida. Today it is called the "Green Swamp."

Fort King was the Indian was the Indian Agency which housed the Indian agent who distributed food, seed, goods, and money to the Seminoles. Ft. King was built on the northern border of the Seminole reservation in 1827. It took a year to clear the land spring (Silver Springs) to build

135

the fort. Ft. King was named for a white plantation owner with the last name of "King." Ironically, he was married to an African queen. A road called Fort Military Road was also built. It connected Ft. King to Ft. Brooke in Tampa.

Many soldiers living in forts in Florida suffered often from fleas, dysentery, and many diseases. One soldier wrote home and said, "If the devil owned both Hell and Florida, he would rent out Florida and live in Hell!" Another soldier, Amos Beebe Eaton, wrote this about Florida in his journal, "Florida was the most barren, sandy, swampy, and good for nothing peninsula...The Seminoles can never be put in a country so much secluded from the white man as here! Leave the deceived Indian, where God placed them!"

One year after taking office as the U.S. president (1831), Andrew Jackson, had passed the Indian Removal Act. The Choctaws, Creeks, Chickasaws, Cherokee, and the Seminoles were to emigrate to the Indian Territory. The territory was located west of the Mississippi River – today known as Oklahoma. The Indians were to go peacefully and voluntarily, however, the Seminoles resisted.

Colonel James Gadsden had orders from Andrew Jackson to help convince the Seminoles to sign the Payne's Landing Treaty and embark to the Indian Territory. The Seminoles would receive $80,000.00 for their land in Florida. Seven Seminole chiefs and eight subchiefs signed the treaty with the stipulation that a delegation of seven Seminoles and Micanopy's interpreter, Abraham, would inspect the territory first. If they approved, and if the tribe accepted their decision when they returned, the treaty would be ratified. Chief Micanopy claimed he never signed the Payne's Landing Treaty.

Seminole leaders that *might* have been part of this delegation to inspect the territory were King Philip, Wildcat, Alligator, Billy Bowlegs, Osceola, Jumper, Abraham, and John Hicks. They left by steamboat at Ft. Brooke in Tampa and journeyed north into the Gulf of Mexico via the Mississippi and Arkansas River systems to Arkansas. From

Arkansas they rode horse back to Fort Gibson. Fort Gibson was similar to a welcome station. The Seminoles were not informed that they would be sharing the Creek Indian land in the territory. They were also not told that the Maroons were to be returned to their former masters. The Seminoles delegation and tribe refused the land in the territory. However, the delegation was tricked into signing the Ft. Gibson Treaty. According to an American soldier, Major Ethan Allen Hitchcock, Abraham was bribed with two hundred dollars to convince the Seminoles to sign the Ft. Gibson Treaty.

About one out of eight Seminoles were willing to leave Florida, because of starvation, and the slave hunters constantly trespassing onto their reservation. There was a time, when many healthy Seminoles lived to be one hundred years old or older, however during this time of war, they were dying younger and younger.

Dade's Ambush/Massacre took place three days after Christmas of 1835. the Seminoles refer to this battle as an "ambush," but the white soldiers refer to it as a "massacre." Major Francis Langhorne Dade and one hundred soldiers and eight officers were attacked along Ft. King Military Road by one hundred eighty Seminoles led by Alligator Warrior. Only three Seminoles were lost and five were wounded. However, all but three white soldiers were killed. On the same day, Osceola attacked and killed the Indian agent, Wiley Thompson, at Ft. King.

A new Indian agent arrived in Florida to relocate the Seminoles to the Indian Territory – General Sidney Jesup. He destroyed Seminole villages and captured many Seminole women, children, elderly, and Maroon Indians. He also stole their livestock. Jesup's tactics finally convinced two hundred plus Seminoles, including chief Micanopy and Alligator Warrior, to relocate to the territory. However, Osceola convinced them and many others to return to the Wahoo Swamp and fight another day. This infuriated Jesup

137

and he decided the only solution was the *extermination* of all Seminoles!

Another new face arrived in Florida – a seventy-year old medicine man from Georgia named Sam Jones. He became known as the "Great Rascal." Jones would not allow his followers to leave Florida. Sam Jones never migrated and was never captured!

On September 9, 1837, King Philip was captured and held prisoner in the old Spanish fort in St. Augustine. There were also seventy-one warriors, six women, and four Maroons. Later King Philip's son, Wildcat, along with Osceola and others were arrested under a white flag of truce, and imprisoned in the Spanish fort too. There were protests up and down the east coast by Americans about the way Jesup captured Osceola. Indian agent, General Sidney Jesup, found himself in the position of having to defend his actions for the rest of his life! Wildcat and nineteen others escaped. Osceola was too ill to travel and stayed behind with two hundred plus loyal followers. They were later transferred to Ft. Moultrie in Charleston, South Carolina, where Osceola later died and was buried.

Alligator Warrior, Wildcat, and Sam Jones led around four hundred Seminoles in battle against Colonel Zachary Taylor, known as "Old Rough and Ready." The Seminoles were outnumbered three to one. The battle took place on Christmas day 1837 and was known as the Battle of Okeechobee. It lasted for almost three hours and ended in a drawl. Taylor claimed victory and was promoted to Brigadier General. Eleven Seminoles died and fourteen were wounded compared to twenty-six U.S. soldiers/volunteers dead and one hundred twelve wounded.

The end of the Second Seminole War was drawing to a close with the capture of Chief Micanopy. Alligator Warrior and eighty-one followers were also captured by General Jesup. The Cherokee Indians had helped bring this group in, again under a white flag of truce. Alligator Warrior escaped and returned to Wildcat in the Wahoo Swamp. Wildcat was later seized at Ft. Pierce, near the Big Cypress Swamp, with fifteen of his warriors. Two hundred fifty Seminoles, along with Alligator Warrior, surrendered forty days later, and followed Wildcat to the Indian Territory, after he spoke to them. ("The Lamentations of Wildcat" – Wildcat's famous speech urging his followers to the Indian Territory.)

The Seminoles were placed on the Creeks' land in the Indian Territory. The territorial Seminoles failed to notice Wildcat's matrilineal birthright to become chief. Instead they named John Jumper, chief in the territory. Wildcat, Alligator Warrior, and Gopher John (a freedman of African, Seminole, and Spanish descent) secretly organized their escape by storing supplies, food and ammunition. Seven years after they had arrived in the Indian Territory they left with one hundred other discontent Seminoles and Maroons. They headed to Mexico. Their trip lasted for one year. The group settled near El Nacimiento. This is where Alligator Warrior's track runs cold. He could have possibly died along the way or later in Mexico, when Wilcat and others died of smallpox in 1857.

Six years later, the Seminole Nation was formed in the Indian Territory, and some of the Seminoles in Mexico returned to the territory. However, the Maroons were not welcome (Tripartite Treaty), and remained in Mexico. Many became known as "Seminole-Negro Scouts" and worked for the U.S. Army. Gopher John became their leader and was given the name "John Horse." Many of the Seminole descendants still live along the Rio Grande River today in Mexico and Texas.

Dictionary - "What did they say?"

The Seminole Indians speak two languages: Muscogee and Miccosukee. Muscogee, originally called musquas, is generally called Seminole and spoken in Oklahoma. The Seminole Miccosukee Indians of Florida call their language Hitchiti. Some Seminoles can speak both languages. My dictionary is made up of both dialects. Many Seminole words are difficult to pronounce there is no "r" sound; it is replaced with the "th" sound. The Seminoles are a soft-spoken people and rarely raise their voice at one another! The Seminoles did not have a written language for many years.

1. Apalachicola – place of the ruling people

2. Alligator –Halpatter or halpata or allapattah (hull-butta)

3. Alligator Town – Halpata Tolophka or Talwa (Tu-low-ba)

4. Aripeka – a Seminole chief

5. Ban (d) – originally a separate tribe; old tribal names were Cheyaha, Kanchatee, Talahassee, Mikasuki, and Muskogee. Ban(d) membership determined by your mother. There are fourteen ban(d)s in Florida today.

6. Big Jug – Alachua (Ala-cue-ah) sinkhole at Payne's Prairie

7. Black Drink – (pa-sa-is-kit-a) brewed from the leaves of holly bushes (cassina plant), it acted like a stimulant because of the caffeine in it. It was used in purification rites.

8. Black Bear – narcoossee or nokosehaco Seminoles believed that bears used to be men. This explains why bears can walk upright.

9. Boy – chebon (chuh-bond)

10. Brother – cuse (ju-se)

11. Canoe – an Indian boat built out of a cypress log; it could possibly hold as many as thirty men and could make trips to the Florida Keys, the Bahamas, and even Cuba.

12. Chickee – traditional housing of the Seminoles; built with a raised floor and no exterior walls. It replaced their log huts when the Seminoles moved into south Florida starting in the 1820's. One chickee was used for sleeping and another for relaxing like a family room.

13. Chief – Micco (Me-co) a Seminole chief could advise but never demand. It was a hereditary position through the mother's lineage.

14. Clan – a large family whose members share a common ancestor. Clan kinship was decided through the mother. Seminole clan names: Raccoon, Bear, Wind, Alligator, Deer, Snake, and Panther. The Panther Clan was the first, and thus, they created the laws. Some clans are extinct today.

15. Corn Soup – sofkee (sof-ka) similar to grits; a hot corn soup often thickened to a stew by adding vegetables and meat

16. Cow – waka (waa-ka)

17. Creek Indians – name given by English explorers to Indians that lived along a creek (Ocheese Creek or Ocmulgee River) in Georgia. Upper Creeks lived in the north and Lower Creeks lived in the south.

18. Deer – echo (ee-cho)

19. Dog – efaw (ef-fa)

20. Emathla – a clan leader or subchief

21. Everglades – pay-hai-o-kee= Great Grass Waters

22. Father – erke (eth-ke)

23. Fish – thlocklo or laa-le

24. Fort – (or grave) tohopki

25. Friend – uh-hiss-see

26. Girl – hoktuce (hok-te)

27. Gold – lani (la-nee) or cvto-kunvp-lane (cha-doe-ko-nop-la-nee)

28. Great Spirit – Pohyah (Poe-hi-uh) or His-a-kit-a-mis-i – the creator; Hesaketa – breath of life; Tumese – giver of life; Many lesser gods, but one great spirit

29. Hadjo – (hay-jo) mad or reckless brave or a title of honor

30. Hello or How are you? – eshtungo (ish-done-go) or estonko

31. Hitchiti – (Hidge-uh-dee) language of the Mikasuki Indians.

32. Immokalee – my camp

33. Indian Agent – U.S. government agent that supplied Indians with payment, seed, food, and/or farm utensils

34. Indian Territory – Between 1817 – 1842 the land designated west of the Mississippi River; Arkansas at that time and Oklahoma today; was the reservation of five eastern U.S. tribes: Cherokee, Choctaw, Seminole, Creek, and Chickasaw.

35. Maroons or Afro-Seminoles – African American slaves that fled slavery and developed their own culture: a mixture of African tradition and adopted Seminole ways of life. Many spoke Gullah (Goulah), a mixture of African, English, Spanish, and Seminole.

36. Micanopy – (Me-cuh-no-bee) top chief; also spelled Mikonopi

37. Micco – (Me-co) chief

38. Mico Apokta – speaker for the chief

39. Mikasuki – (Mic-uh-su-kee) the unconquered people

40. Mother – etske or itski (itch- ke)

41. Muskogee or Muscogee – (Muh-sko-gee) Seminoles known as the Cow Creek Indians

42. Nakita – "What is it?"

43. Neharakkoce – (Ni-ha-tak-ko-ci) Little Big Fat (Seminole name)

44. No – hegosh or monks

45. Nokin – "I don't know"

46. Okeechobee – big water

47. Olustee – brackish water

48. Orange– ya-laahe

49. Owl– opa

50. Palatka – ferry crossing or crossing at river

51. Panther– coo-wah-chobee or katcalani

52. Pasaiskita – black drink drank as a cleansing ritual at the Green Corn Dance

53. Patriot – Americans living in Spanish Florida; wanted Florida to become a U.S. territory.

54. Pig – sho-ke

55. Powwow – Indian social gathering; today usually a tourist attraction

56. Prairie – hialeah

57. Rabbit – cho-fo-lock-sah

58. Renegade – a trader or turncoat

59. Reservation – U.S. government land designated for Indian tribes; today more than 2,000 Florida Seminoles live on six reservations located at Hollywood, Big Cypress, Brighton, Immokalee, Ft. Pierce, and Tampa.

60. Seminole – (or spelled Siminoles) word origin Spanish – "Cimarron(es) which can mean free people or wild people and the Muskogee word "se-mi-no-li" means runaway. Seminole Indians today prefer the meaning "pioneer" or "adventurer." William Bartram a traveler and botanist described the Seminole appearance in his published travel log (1774) – "Perfect human figure, (average height 6'4) the forehead and brows so formed as to strike you instantly with heroism and bravery; the eye though rather small, yet active and full of fire."

61. Sensebearer – speaker of the tribe

62. Sister – cvcuse (cha-ju-se)

63. Smoke mokke (mok-ki)

L.L. Eadie

64. Snake – chitto or cektohaco (cik-to-ha-co) or chente; Rattlesnake – cetto-mekko

65. Soluthoke – Lying on the Ground Creeping (Seminole name)

66. Spring – Ocala

67. Squirrel – hen-le

68. Suwannee (Suwahnee) – river of reeds

69. Tampa – place of drifwood

70. Teattokonawa – (teat-to-ko-na-wa) stone beads used as money; teattokonawa hatki – silver beads; teattokonawa lani – gold beads

71. Teayaiyaktsi – Hush Be Quiet (Seminole name)

72. Thank you – mvto (ma-doe)

73. Turtle – yok-che; Box Turtle – yuk-che-po-luk-skit

74. Tustenuggee – (tus-tuh-nug-ge) a subchief; a highest warrior title bestowed on a warrior for his performance on the battlefield. The chief and his council select the tustenuggee.

75. Uncle – Pavwa (po-wa)

76. "We will meet again" – e-de-he-ja-kaw-des

77. White person – este hvtke

78. Yes – ehhe (eh-uh-hey)

Character Reference - "Who's Who?"

1. <u>Abiaka (a-be-ka) a.k.a. Sam Jones</u> – Seminole Miccosukee Medicine Man originally from Georgia who was a staunch resister of removal to the Indian Territory. He was in his seventies at the beginning of the Second Seminole War. He used his medicine to stir the warriors into frenzy. He was never captured and was known as the "great rascal." He lived to be one hundred years old in the Florida Everglades. He died in 1867 in south Florida. Every Seminole in Florida was present at the time of his death. Some because they loved him and others because they feared him. He is credited for the presence of Seminoles in Florida today.

2. <u>Abraham (Souanakki Tustenukle) or "Old Abram"</u> – (1790-1870) Born a slave and owned by Dr. Sierra of Pensacola, Fl. Later he became Micanopy's slave and advisor/interpreter during the Second Seminole War. He was a powerful Maroon leader. His village was called "Abraham's Old Town or Peliklikaha." It was the largest Maroon village with about one hundred runaway Georgia slaves. It was located in Bushnell, Florida in Sumpter County, ten miles west of Dade's Battlefield. Abraham's village was burnt to the ground in 1836 by U.S. troops. He became a paid guide and interpreter for the U.S. Army.

3. <u>Alligator Warrior (Halpatter Tustenuggee) a.k.a. Chief Alligator</u> – One of Chief Micanopy's right hand men. He had great influence on his chief and planned the first major Seminole victory during the Second Seminole War called Dade's Massacre or Ambush. He continued to resist until his ultimate capture and deportation to the Indian Territory in 1841. He migrated to Mexico along with Wildcat's followers from the Indian Territory.

4. <u>Billy Bowlegs (Holatta Micco or Holata Mico)</u> – Seminole leader in the Third Seminole War also called the Bowlegs' War. He surrendered in 1858 and was sent to the Indian

Territory. He and his band were the last group deported from Florida. He died shortly after his arrival there. He was Micanopy's nephew.

5. <u>Black Snake</u> – fictional Maroon tustenuggee

6. <u>Bowlegs (Bolek)</u> – King Payne's brother and leader of the Seminoles near Latchaway (Alachua), after being attacked he moved his band near the Suwannee River (Bowlegs' Town). He died in 1821.

7. <u>Coacoochee (Coo-wah-kah-chee) Wildcat or a.k.a. the Red Knight</u> – son of King Philip, born about 1807, his mother was the sister of Micanopy. He was known for his flamboyant personality and extravagant dress…possibly because he wore Shakespearian costumes he had taken from a traveling play troope headed to St. Augustine, that he had attacked. He took not only their costumes but also their sets as well. He was deported to the Indian Territory in 1841. He later left and migrated to Mexico. He became a colonel in the Mexican army and died there in 1857 of smallpox.

8. <u>Cowkeeper a.k.a. Seacoffee</u> – came to Florida with James Oglethorpe with a force of 2000 whites and a large number of Lower Creeks. He was a Lower Creek Indian and son of Emperor Brims of the Creek Nation in southern Alabama and Georgia. Oglethorpe, from Savannah, Georgia employed the Creeks to help attack St. Augustine in 1740. Cowkeeper must have decided to stay in Florida and settled near Gainesville. He herded the free ranging herds of cattle from an abandoned Spanish ranch called "La Chua." He later founded Cuscowilla, fifteen miles south of Gainesville. He died in 1784 and was succeeded by his nephew, King Payne.

9. <u>Gold (Lani)</u> – fictional little person and good luck charm for Alligator Warrior

10. <u>Governor William P. DuVal</u> - appointed governor of the Florida territory in 1822 (-1834). He did try to improve the conditions of the Seminole Indians. During flooding he increased their food allotment but ordered that no whites

could purchase their livestock. The whites also could not trade with the Indians unless they received a license from an Indian agent or DuVal.

11. <u>Hawk Eyes or Little Big Fat (Neharakkoce)</u> – Alligator's fictional fellowhood brother/friend

12. <u>Hush Be Quiet (Teayaiyaktsi)</u> – fictional wife of Hawk Eyes

13. <u>James Gadsden</u> – friend and former aide to Andrew Jackson. He was selected by Jackson to conduct the negotiations with the Seminoles on the Indian Removal Act. County in west Florida named "Gadsden."

14. <u>Gohper John (a.k.a. Juan Caballo or Cavala = Spanish for John Horse)</u> – He was a freedman of African, Indian, and Spanish ancestry. He was also Wildcat's interpreter and a Maroon chief. He left with Wildcat and Alligator Warrior for Mexico from the Indian Territory. In Mexico he fought bravely with the Mexican army and became known as El Coronel Juan Caballo. The Mexican army awarded him with a silver saddle which had a gold-plated horses's head in place of the horn on the saddle. He used this beautiful saddle while riding his horse, "American." He was an excellent horseman.

15. <u>John Hicks (Tuko-See Mathla)</u> – was an important Miccosukee chief of the Wind and Panther Clans. When an election was held and organized by the U.S. government to select a Chief of the Three Nations: Miccosukee, Seminoles, and Tallahassees---he was selected. Many Indians felt the vote had been rigged by the U.S. government because Hicks was pro-Indian Territory. He died mysteriously. The Seminoles believed in hereditary rule…Micanopy was their chief. Micanopy had also been on the ballot.

16. <u>Andrew Jackson (a.k.a. Old Hickory and Sharp Knife)</u> – He was from Tennessee and was the first American governor of Florida. He was a forceful supporter of the Indian Removal Act. He believed the Indians were like children and needed guidance. He believed this removal would be to their benefit.

It would allow the Indians to resettle in an area where they could govern themselves and live in peace. During the First Seminole War, Jackson burned Indians towns, captured African Maroons, and hung a Medicine Man. He later became the president of the United States. A year later he pushed for the Indian Removal Act.

17. General Thomas Sidney Jesup – was sent to Florida by the U.S. government to end the Second Seminole War. During the time in which he was in command he captured 1,978 Seminoles and 400 more were killed. He did more than any other American general had done to end the war but because of his improper methods of seizure (ex. Captured Osceola under a white flag of truce) he deserves no acclaim. His explanation was that the capture was more humane than being hunted down in the woods like an animal.

18. Jumper (a.k.a. Otee Amathla or Hote-mathla which means "Home Warrior") was a former Red Stick Indian who married the sister or his chief, Micanopy. He became the chief's sensekeeper or private counselor. He was the speaker of the tribe and therefore spoke on Micanopy's behalf.

19. John Jumper (Micco Nutchasa) – Seminole chief in the Indian Territory. He was born in Florida about 1820 and taken prisoner to the Indian Territory around 1843. When he died in 1896 the chief of the Choctaws, another territorial tribe, said this about his death, "Like the fall of a mighty tree in the stillness of the forest."

20. Kickapoos – originally called the Kiikaapoa Indians; they were the tribe from the west that settled with the Seminoles in Mexico.

21. Long Tom (Solachoppo) – King Payne's nephew that followed Bowlegs (Bolek) as Seminole Chief. Long Tom's brother was Micanopy which followed him as chief after his short reign.

22. Micanopy or Micconapy or Mico Onapa = Chief (a.k.a. Sint-Chahkee = Pond Governor) – He was one of the most

important chiefs of the Seminoles. His uncle was King Payne of Payne's Prairie. He rarely gave orders but instead depended on his staff: Abraham, Jumper, Alligator, King Philip, and Holartoochee (who had been banished for four years for adultery; however he did later become one of Micanopy's war leaders.

23. Moses – fictional Maroon friend of Alligator

24. Neamathla – a former Red Stick from Georgia (Fowltown); his tribe was the first attacked during the First Seminole War. He was chosen by the Seminole leaders as their negotiator at the Moultrie Creek Treaty meeting in 1823. His band later left Florida and rejoined the Creeks in Alabama.

25. Osceola or Asseholar or Asi-Yaholo = "one who sings out" or "black drink singer" (the cry of those drinking the black drink---pasaiskita) – was a key war leader duing the Second Seminole War and vowed to fight "till the last drop of Seminole blood had moistened the dust of his hunting ground!" He was captured while under a flag of truce and later died while imprisoned at Ft. Moultrie, South Carolina. His childhood name was Billy Powell. His father was an Englishman named William Powell and his mother was a Red Stick Creek Indian. His great-grandfather was from Scotland. It is said he had the mixed blood of English, Scottish, Irish, Indian, and African.

26. King Payne – He was either the son or nephew of Chief Cowkeeper. He followed Cowkeeper in 1784 as chief. He lived in a typical southern plantation home with slaves and livestock. His brother was Bowlegs. When King Payne was killed in 1813 at the age of eighty by Colonel Daniel Newnan and his troops, Bowlegs said this at his brother's funeral, "What is passed and cannot be prevented should not be grieved for. What a misfortune for me that I could not have died this day, instead of you. What a trifling loss our people would have sustained in my death; how great in yours! I shall wrap you in a robe and hoist you to a slender scaffold where the whistling winds shall take your spirit to the happy hunting

grounds." King Payne was succeeded by his brother, Bowlegs. Payne's Prairie state preserve is named in his honor. It is located between Gainesville and Ocala, Florida.

27. <u>King Philip (a.k.a. Emathla)</u> – he was the chief of a band of Mikasukis that lived along the St. Johns River. He had married the sister of Chief Micanopy and his son was the famous Coacoochee or Wildcat. King Philip was captured and imprisoned in St. Augustine after his slave led the U.S. troops to his camp.

28. <u>Seminoles –</u> originally called themselves "Ikanyuksalgi" which means in Muskogee, "people of the peninsula." The Spanish called them the "Cimmarones" or "free people.' The U.S. citizens called them the "Seminoles." Most were originally the Creek Indians from Alabama and Georgia that had been forced from their homes into Florida. However, they also had roots in the following Indian tribes: Hitchita, Apalachee, Mikasuki, Choctaw, Apalachicola, and Oconee. The Seminoles of Florida were also joined by runaway slaves. The Seminoles and the Maroons vowed that no white man would own them.

29. <u>Zachary Taylor (aka Old Rough and Ready)</u> fought Alligator, Wildcat, and Sam Jones to a drawl at the Battle of Okeechobee. Taylor claimed a victory and was rewarded with a promotion to Brigadier General four years later. He was elected president of the United States in 1849 and only served sixteen months; died while in office.

Timeline - "When Did It Happen?"

1795   Birth of Alligator in south Georgia

1808   Importation of slaves into United States is forbidden

1812   Georgia volunteers led by Colonel Daniel Newnan attack Seminoles in north Florida killing King Payne

1813   Seminoles attacked by Tenneessee mounted volunteers; Alligator moves his village south; Osceola, age nine comes to Florida with his mother and his uncle; Creek War (1813-1814)

1814   Battle of Horseshoe Bend

1816   First Seminole War (1816-1818)

1817   Township of Alligator (Halpata Tolophka) chartered

1818   Spain sold Florida to U.S. for $5 million

1821   Florida is transferred from Spain to U.S.; Andrew Jackson is first Florida governor; approximately 7,000 Seminoles in Florida Treaty of Moultrie Creek; U.S. recognizes Seminole tribe as an Indian Nation

1827   Florida Legislature decrees that any male Seminole found off the Reservation shall receive not exceeding thirty-nine stripes on his bare back and his gun conviscated

1830   Indian Removal Act

1832   Treaty of Payne's Landing; seven Indian leaders visit Indian Territory; creation of Columbia County Florida – boyhood home of Alligator Warrior

1833   Treaty of Fort Gibson (March 28); U.S. Post Officed established in Alligator Town, Fl.

1835   Second Seminole War (1835-1842); Dade Ambush/Massacre; death of Indian agent, Wiley Thompson; Battle of Withlacoochee; Alligator Town (Halpata Tolophka) named county seat in Fl.

1836   (March 6) cease-fire signed at Ft. Dade by: Jumper, Davy Elliot, Cloud, and Alligator (acting on behalf of their chief, Micanopy), agreed to emigrate to the Indian Territory by April 10, 1837 at Fort Brooke (Tampa)

1837   Seminole Indian chief King Philip captured by U.S. troops; Osceola and 80 warriors captured under a white flag of truce; Battle of Okeechobee

1838   Micanopy and Alligator captured and held at Ft. Brooke (Tampa); Alligator escapes; Seminole chief, Micanopy deported to Indian Territory

1841   Osceola dies in captivity at Ft. Moultrie in Charleston, South Carolina; Capture/deportation of Wildcat along with Alligator and majority of his band; others retreat to Everglades

1842   Second Seminole War ends without a treaty (U.S. government had spent $40 million and lost 1,500 soldiers) "Armed Occupation Act of 1842" (200,000 acres) gave 10,000 white settlers eighteen years or older and able to bear arms – 160 acres in north Florida. To obtain the title the settler had to reside on the land for five years, build a house, and farm at least five acres. The settlement had to take place within one year.

1843   Alligator Warrior and a Seminole delegation (including Wildcat) lobbied Washington D.C. for improved conditions with Creek Indians in the Indian Territory

1845   Tripartite Treaty – forced Seminoles to share land with Creeks, stipulated that Seminoles slaves had to be returned to their white masters; Florida joins the Union – 27th state

1849-(1850?) Alligator Warrior, Wildcat, Gopher John, and Seminole followers secretly leave the Indian Territory reservation and head to Mexico; A white man fishing along the Indian River in Florida is killed by a group of Seminoles = provoked the Third Seminole War in Fl.

1855   Third Seminole War a.k.a. The Billy Bowlegs War

1856   Seminoles in the Indian Territory given their own land separate from the Creeks (2,170,000 acres); established the first Seminole Nation in Oklahoma

1858   End of Third Seminole War; Billy Bowlegs is captured and sent with 164 Seminoles from Florida to the Indian Territory; ended the U.S. attempt to remove Seminoles from Florida

1859   Alligator Town (Halpata Tolophka) is incorporated as Lake City, Florida

1861   Civil War begins (ends 1865) Seminole Nation splits

1866   Second Seminole Nation formed in Oklahoma separate from Florida

1916   Colorful patchwork designed clothing created by Seminole women using hand-cranked sewing machines

1957   Seminole tribe improved their independence by adopting the Seminole Constitution (this established the federally recognized Seminole Tribe of Florida)

1970   The Indian Claims Commission awarded the Seminoles of both Florida and Oklahoma collectively $12,347,500 for the land taken from them by the U.S. Military. However, it failed to specify how the money was to be divided between the two groups; ended up in courts

1990   Twenty years later the dispute was settled; $50 million Seminole land claims was divided 75% to Seminoles in Oklahoma and 25% to Florida Seminoles

L.L. Eadie

Bibliography - "How Do You Know That?"

The author wishes to express her appreciation to the following references for their great wealth of information. She encourages her readers to peruse these valuable references.

1. Atlas of Florida, University Press of Fl., Gainesville, Fl., copyright 1992 revised 1996.

2. Born of the Sun, Fl. Bicentennial Commemorative Journal, Inc., Hollywood, Fl., copyright 1975.

3. Dade Battlefield State Historic Site Brochure

4. Dade's Last Command, by Frank Laumer, University Press of Fl., Gainesville, Fl., copyright 1995.

5. The Enduring Seminoles: From Alligator Wrestling to Ecotourism, by Patsy West, University Press of Fl., copyright 1998.

6. Everglades, by Jean Craighead George, Harper Collins Publishers, USA, copyright 1995.

7. Florida's Indians from Ancient Times to the Present, by Jerald T. Milanich, University Press of Fl., Gainesville, Fl., copyright 1998.

8. Florida News for Alumni and Friends of the U.F., vol. 2, Jan. 2002, "In Search of Maroons," p. 5.

9. Gopher, Lorine, Brighton Reservation, @ Jenny Shore, Lake Okeechobee, Fl.

10. The History of Columbia County Florida, by Edward F. Keuchel, Hunter Printing Co., Lake City, Fl., copyright 1996.

11. Legends of the Seminoles by Betty Mae Jumper, Pineapple Press, Inc., Sarasota, Fl., copyright 1994.

12. Osceola, Peggy, Seminole Okalee Indian Village and Museum, 5845 S. St. Rd. Seven, Ft. Lauderdale, Fl., 33314.

13. Osceola's Legacy, Patricia R. Wickman, The University of Alabama Press, Tucaloosa, AL., copyright 1991.

14. The Seminoles of Florida, by James W. Covington, University Press of Fl., Gainesville, Fl., copyright 1993.

15. Seminoles Days of Long Ago, by Kenneth W. Mulder, Mulder Enterprises, Publisher, Tampa Bay, Fl., copyright Dec. 1991.

16. The Seminole Indians, by Philip Koslow, Chelsea House Pub., printed in Mexico, copyright 1994.

17. The Seminole Indians of Florida, by Clay MacCauley, University Press of Fl., Gainesville, Fl., copyright 2000.

18. The Story of Florida's Seminole Indians, by Wilfred T. Neill, Great Outdoors Publishing Co., St. Petersburg, Fl., copyright 1956.

19. Spain, Dmman, a.k.a. Little Shot, Seminole Nation of Oklahoma Historic Preservation Office, P.O. Box 1498, Wewoka, Ok. 74884

20. Unconquered People: Florida's Seminole and Miccosukee Indians, by Brent Richards Weisman, University Press of Fl., Gainesville, Fl., Copyright 1999.

21. http://www.aboutnorthgeorgia.com/ang/Creek_Nation, History of the Creek Nation-American Indians in North Georgia, Golden Ink, copyright 1994-2000.

22. http://sites.google.com/archerhistoricalsociety/history-of-archer-fl/19-century-archer/braley_manuscript/ Ninteenth Century Archer, by Rance O. Braley

23. https://dos.myflorida.com/florida-facts/florida-history/seminole-history/seminole-leaders/ Seminole Leaders, Fl. Dept. of State, Katherine Harris, Secretary of State, Division of Historical Resources.

24. https://www.semtribe.com/STOF/history/introduction. Florida of the Seminoles.

25. http://paranormalghostsociety.org/Fort%20King%20Burial%20Grou nd.htm. Chief John Hicks, by Chris Chris Kimball, 1998.

26. https://en.wikipedia.org/wiki/Alachua_County,_Florida - Alachua County

L.L. Eadie

27. https://en.wikipedia.org/wiki/Madison_County,_Florida - Madison County

28. http://www.ourgeorgiahistory.com/indians/Creek/creek01.html, History of the Creek Nation-American Indians in North Georgia, by Larry Worthy, editor in chief.

29. https://en.wikipedia.org/wiki/Wild_Cat(Seminole) The Lamentations of Wildcat (Coacoochee).

30. http://scholar.library.miami.edu/Eaton/ A Soldier's Journal of the Second Seminole Indian War, July 31, 1837- Aug. 24, 1838.

31. https://www.pbs.org/ Judgement Day: Indian Removal 1814-1858 Africans in America.

32. https://en.wikipedia.org/wiki/Seminole_Nation_of_Oklahoma/ Seminole Nation of Oklahoma, Historic Preservation Office.

33. https://semtribe.com/stof - Seminole Tribe of Florida: History, Hollywood, Fl., copyright 1997-2000.

34. https://semtribe.com/stof - Culture:Language.

35. https://guides.loc.gov/indian-removal-act. The Indian Removal Act of 1830, author U.S. gov't.

36. https://en.wikipedia.org/wiki/List_of_chiefs_of-the_Seminoles - Seminole Nation Leaders: Chiefs and Governors, by LaDonna Sims.

37. http://strangemag.com/ogopogp.html   Nessie and Other Monsters by Mark Chorvinsky.

38. https://digital.utsa.edu/digital/api/collection/p15125coll4/id/485/download - They Came From Florida: The Seminole Indian Scouts,Mexico

39. http://texasindians.com - Black Seminole Indians.

40. https://www.omniglot.com/writing/creek.htm - Creek Indian Language Dictionary

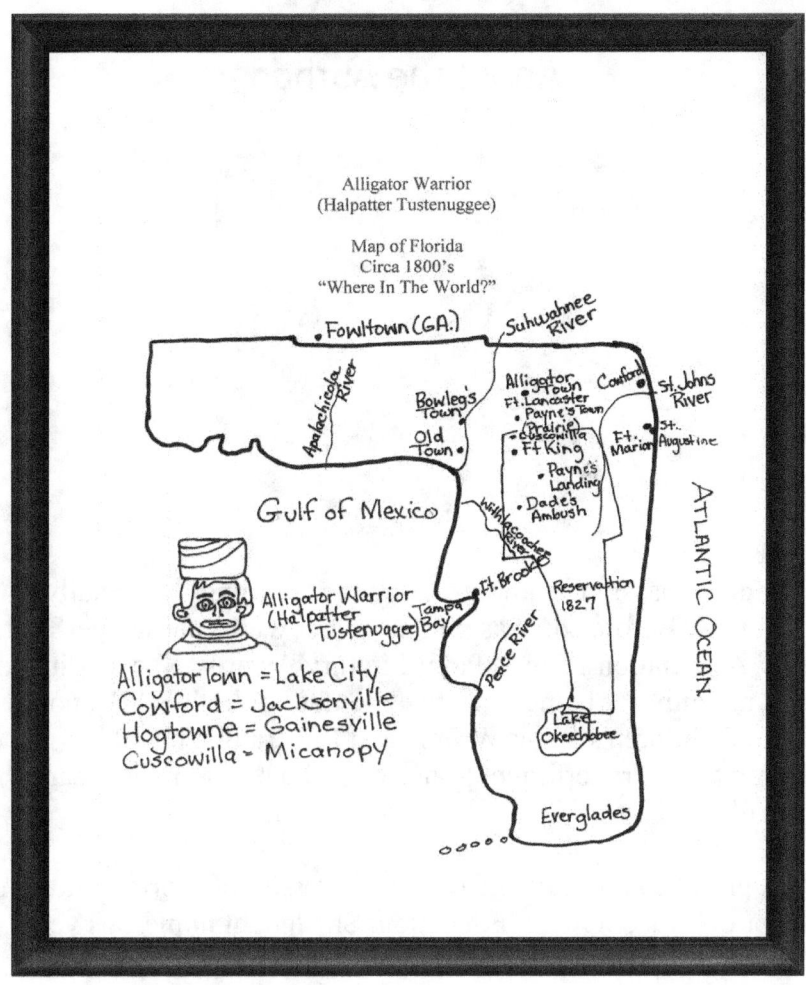

Alligator Warrior
(Halpatter Tustenuggee)

Map of Florida
Circa 1800's
"Where In The World?"

Fowltown (GA.)

Suhwahnee River

Apalachicola River

Bowleg's Town

Old Town

Alligator Town
Ft. Lancaster
Payne's Town
(Prairie)
Cuscowilla
Ft King
Payne's Landing
Dade's Ambush
Withlacoochee

Cowford

St. Johns River

Ft. Marion

St. Augustine

Gulf of Mexico

Alligator Warrior
(Halpatter Tustenuggee)

Tampa Bay

Ft. Brooke

Reservation 1827

Peace River

ATLANTIC OCEAN

Lake Okeechobee

Alligator Town = Lake City
Cowford = Jacksonville
Hogtowne = Gainesville
Cuscowilla = Micanopy

Everglades

157

About the Author

L. L. Eadie is passionate about writing and reading - especially for young adults. Before she was published her works earned her Florida Writers' Association's Royal Palm Literary Awards. She credits her success not only for being an active member of both FWA and the Society of Children's Book Writers and Illustrators, but also belonging to several critique groups over the past ten plus years she's been writing.

She is a proud Gator graduate of the University of Florida - holding a Bachelor of Arts degree in Education. She taught numerous years, grades, subjects, and children.

She is inspired daily and often nightly when her muse wakes her with a fabulous new idea or pressing story to be written.

To get in contact with the author check out her website and social media pages.

Facebook Page: https://www.facebook.com/L-L-Eadie-141069182765272/

Twitter Account: https://twitter.com/lindaeadie

Amazon Profile Page: https://www.amazon.com/-/e/B084M7TK7T

Website: https://lindaeadie.wixsite.com/booksbylleadie/

YouTube Channel: https://www.youtube.com/channel/UCOqwdnT40rPwg7HSE6GmKl g

Email: LLEadieauthor@gmail.com